THE DOLL'S EYE

BY **MARINA COHEN**
ILLUSTRATIONS BY **NICOLETTA CECCOLI**

SQUARE
FISH

ROARING BROOK PRESS / NEW YORK

SQUARE
FISH

An imprint of Macmillan Publishing Group, LLC
175 Fifth Avenue, New York, NY 10010
mackids.com

Our books may be purchased in bulk for promotional, educational, or
business use. Please contact your local bookseller or the Macmillan Corporate
and Premium Sales Department at (800) 221-7945 ext. 5442 or by
email at MacmillanSpecialMarkets@macmillan.com.

Library of Congress Cataloging-in-Publication Data

Names: Cohen, Marina, 1967–   author.
Title: The doll's eye / by Marina Cohen; illustrations by Nicoletta Ceccoli
Description: New York : Roaring Brook Press, 2017. | Summary: "The day
    Hadley discovers the lone glass eye in the empty attic of her new house
    is the day her life changes forever"—Provided by publisher.
Identifiers: LCCN 2016009080 (print) | LCCN 2016036033 (ebook) |
    ISBN 978-1-250-14396-9 (paperback) | ISBN 978-1-62672-205-7 (ebook)
Subjects: | CYAC: Dolls—Fiction. | Families—Fiction. | Demonology—
    Fiction. | Horror stories. | BISAC: JUVENILE FICTION / Action &
    Adventure / General. | JUVENILE FICTION / Social Issues / Death &
    Dying. | JUVENILE FICTION / Social Issues / Friendship.
Classification: LCC PZ7.1.C64 Do 2017 (print) | LCC PZ7.1.C64 (ebook) |
    DDC [Fic]—dc23
LC record available at https://lccn.loc.gov/2016009080

Originally published in the United States by Roaring Brook Press
First Square Fish edition, 2019
Square Fish logo designed by Filomena Tuosto

1 3 5 7 9 10 8 6 4 2

AR: 4.7 / LEXILE: 680L

For Emily

One

Hadley saw the house on Orchard Drive for the first time the day she moved in.

It was set far back along a sloping dead-end street. Tall and looming, the red brick was faded, the wood trim weathered with age. Through the haze of August heat, it appeared blurred, like an old photograph, ghostly, out of focus. The neighboring homes were smaller and newer. They reminded Hadley of shiny white mushrooms springing up around a great decomposing log. It was only a short drive from their old apartment in the city, but it felt like another world.

Her arms ached under the strain of the box she carried. It was piled high with her books and knickknacks. She adjusted the weight and then climbed the creaky porch steps, pausing a moment at the door, its black paint blistered and chipped. She took a deep breath, nudged it open, and stepped inside.

"It's a dream come true!" Her mother's voice echoed from the kitchen down the long empty hall.

"Sure is," said Ed.

Her mother whispered something and then giggled. She never used to giggle before she met Ed. Now she giggled all the time.

Isaac's head peeked over the upper railing. "Hey, Haddy! There's an attic full of junk! And an old root cellar around the back! Wanna check it out?"

She forced a smile and nodded. "Later." And then he was gone again. Isaac was six, exactly half Hadley's age.

Hadley's gaze curled up the dark oak banister and lingered near the high ceiling. Her grin melted like warm wax down the side of a candlestick. She should be in love with the house. Crazy in love with it. Like Mom and Ed and Isaac. Only something about it felt odd. A heaviness in the air seemed to press down on her. And, despite the August heat, it was cold and clammy, like a years-unopened tomb. She set the box at her feet, turned on her heels, and raced back outside.

Her mother's car was crammed with everything they'd been able to squeeze into it. Still, it seemed like so little. Hadley couldn't help but think of all the things she couldn't fit into a box—her school, her friends, all the familiar people and places. Their tiny apartment had been so full. How could twelve years of memories, mementos, and meaningful moments be reduced to a couple dozen boxes and a handful of suitcases?

Ed's white van was parked behind Mom's car. Bulky duffel bags spilled out of the rear. Inside, between the various ladders, tarps, paint canisters, and brushes, there was a set of golf clubs, a greasy tool kit, countless pairs of running shoes, a fire extinguisher, a jumble of cables, and a blue cooler. All his and Isaac's things would soon mingle with hers and Mom's. Hadley couldn't bear the thought.

She backed away from the driveway and slunk to the edge of the lawn, plunking herself at the curb. She picked up a stick and began etching a circle into the dry dirt while more snippets of excited conversation drifted toward her through the door she'd left ajar.

"...Lovely Linen...or how about Desert Dusk? That's the color Hadley and I painted our old place..."

Hadley gripped the stick tighter. She added a sad mouth to the circle. "Our old place," she muttered, poking two deep, cavernous eyes.

Suddenly, a cascade of spiders rained down around her. She yelped, sprang to her feet, and flung the stick aside. She danced in circles, shaking her scraggly brown hair, slapping frantically at her stomach and bare legs.

"Quit stomping," said a voice. "You'll hurt them."

3

Hadley stopped jumping long enough to see a bulky boy with sandy brown hair standing close behind her.

"Don't just stand there!" she shouted. "Get them off me!"

He reached for her shoulder and gently cupped a spindly legged creature in his hand. He placed it on the ground and let it amble away. He examined her thoroughly and then nodded. "That was the last."

"Who are you?" demanded Hadley, still flicking her hair and patting down her T-shirt. "And what are you doing here?"

"I'm Gabe," he said, extending a hand. "I live five houses down. With my grandma." He grinned sheepishly.

Hadley studied the boy's filthy fingernails, his sooty cheeks, and his button-down shirt two sizes too small. Then her eyes grew wide as they settled on the empty glass jar at his feet and the lid dangling from his fingertips.

"You!" she said, pointing an incredulous finger. "You threw them on me!"

Gabe's cheeks flushed. "Did not." He narrowed his green eyes and raised his chin. "The lid came loose."

Hadley gritted her teeth and frowned. "Well, even if that's true, what were you doing hanging over my shoulder with a jar of spiders anyway?"

"I saw you digging," he said quietly. "I thought you might be looking for grubs."

"Grubs?" she spluttered. "Why would I be looking for *grubs?"*

"It seemed like a logical conclusion at the time." He reached over and lightly brushed another tiny spider from her T-shirt sleeve.

"For the record," said Hadley, "I have zero interest in spiders, grubs, or any other insect you care to drop on me."

He cleared his throat. "Well, technically, spiders aren't insects. They're arachnids."

Hadley threw her hands into the air and huffed loudly. Before she stomped back toward the house, she caught sight of the face she'd drawn in the dirt. Though somewhat trampled, it was still clear. Except the frown she'd drawn had somehow morphed into a smile.

Over her shoulder she heard Gabe call, "I hope you stay longer than the others!"

Two

Give it a chance, Haddy," said her mother. "It's only been a week. We're going to be happy here. Very happy. You'll see." She set two grocery bags at her feet and stretched her arms.

Hadley kicked at the heavy wooden door. It slammed shut with a hollow thud. She sighed loudly for dramatic effect, then noticed her mother had already picked up a bag of groceries and disappeared into the kitchen.

She snatched up the other bag, raced after her, and dumped the contents onto the counter—a loaf of rice bread, a jar of soy butter, some polenta cookies, and five cans of green peas. She plopped herself into a seat at the table and sighed again.

After her mother cleared away the fruit, vegetables, meat, and various packages, she retrieved two slices of rice bread and opened the jar of soy butter. She began making

Hadley a sandwich. Isaac was allergic to peanuts, tree nuts, eggs, shellfish, wheat, and dairy. They couldn't keep any of that stuff in the house.

"I can't even taste the difference," said her mother, smoothing a large glob of yellow-brown paste over the cardboard-like crust.

"I can," mumbled Hadley.

She began tapping her foot to the rhythm of one of her mother's favorite songs.

They'd always made a game of it. She tapped and her mother had to guess the song. Only this time her mother didn't seem to notice, so Hadley stood and began stomping her feet loudly, flapping her arms like a nettled chicken.

"Don't scuff up the floor," said her mother over her shoulder.

Hadley's limbs wilted. She slouched back into her seat while her mother poured a tall glass of orange juice. Orange was Isaac's favorite.

"Hey, wanna do each other's nails?"

"Great idea," said her mother without looking up.

Hadley sprang into action. Her mouth and feet moved at the same time. "I've got some of that purple crackle polish you like and a bunch of the tiny jewels you gave me for my birthday. I saved the blue ones for you. I can probably dig them out of one of the boxes . . ." She made it halfway to the hall.

"Oh," said her mother, glancing over her shoulder. "Did you mean *now*?"

Hadley turned slowly. Her body deflated like a punctured bicycle tire.

"I can't right now." Her mother picked up the plate and the glass. "Ed and Isaac are trying to get that kite to fly. And I'm going to help."

She said it matter-of-factly, as though it were the most natural thing in the world, when she had never expressed the least interest in kites in the past.

The past. That place that seemed so far away. That place when it was only Hadley and her mother. No stepdad named Ed. No stepbrother named Isaac. And no big old creaky house that smelled like a closet full of musty clothes.

Hadley tried to swallow her disappointment, but like a red rubber ball it bounced back up. "Can't they do it on their own? It's not exactly rocket science."

"Come out with us," said her mother. She placed the sandwich and the glass of juice on the table. "It'll be fun."

Hadley glared at the allergen-free sandwich, willing it to explode. She shook her head, blinked hard, and then did a quick about-face.

"Your lunch," said her mother.

Hadley headed for the stairs, taking the steps two at a time.

"We're a family now," called her mother. "Sooner or later you're going to have to get used to it."

Hadley reached the upper landing, raced into her bedroom, and collapsed onto her bed. "Family," she echoed. The word was thick and syrupy. It seeped into the chalky walls, leaving a stain of silence. She closed her eyes.

Things weren't so bad, she told herself. Isaac was kind of cute—when he wasn't barging into her room, asking her silly questions, and messing with her stuff. And Ed wasn't an ax murderer or anything—he just had the personality of gelatinous zooplankton. The house *was* big. And they had gotten it really cheap in a bank auction. And it had come completely furnished. Hadley's mother claimed that was the luckiest part, though it made Hadley feel like a guest in someone else's home.

Suddenly, goose bumps skittered across Hadley's arms, and she got the distinct feeling she was being watched. Her eyes snapped open and swept the room. Nothing but her new-used furniture and her unpacked boxes of junk filled the space. Carefully, she leaned over and peered under the bed. Dust bunnies scampered in all directions.

She was about to hoist herself up when slowly, steadily, out of the darkest corner, something rolled toward her. It made a long drawn-out rumble against the old hardwood floor, stopping just below her face.

Staring up at Hadley was an eye.

Three

Hadley picked up the eye and dusted it off. It was smooth and cold, like a stone long buried beneath ice. It reminded her of a cat's-eye marble—only instead of being clear with colored swirls, it was white with a pale blue iris that contained a million silver folds. It might belong to a stuffed animal, she decided. Or a doll.

Hadley searched her room, but there were no mysterious one-eyed toys lurking in the shadows of the closet or hiding deep inside the dresser drawers.

The side door slammed. Faint sounds drifted in through the open window.

A tiny voice inside Hadley whispered, *I should go out with them.* She turned the eye over and over between her fingertips. *I don't want to go. But I should. I should go. But I don't want to . . .*

The argument whirled inside her mind like a carnival ride until she felt dizzy. She tucked the eye into the pocket of her denim shorts and flopped onto her bed, silencing the voice and steadying her thoughts.

Hadley missed her apartment in Pittsburgh. She missed the white noise of the traffic that lulled her to sleep. She missed the city people who minded their own business. And she especially missed her best friend, Sydney, who'd promised she'd come by just as soon as she got home from Camp Greenly Lake. Hadley even missed Crazy Grace, her mother's kooky friend from the apartment down the hall.

Grace called herself psychic. Others called her batty. She was always warning people not to step on the gnomes in her front garden. Thing was, there was no front garden in the narrow hallway of the old building, and Hadley could say with a fair amount of certainty there were no gnomes. Still, she always made a point of tiptoeing a wide berth around Grace's door frame just in case. The last thing she wanted to be accused of was trampling defenseless invisible gnomes.

Grace would get these premonitions. Like the time she'd whispered to Hadley, "Don't drink the milk." Hadley had no clue what Grace had meant until three weeks later when she got a carton out of the fridge and poured herself a tall glass of cottage-cheesy lumps.

The day they had moved out of the apartment, Grace had

stopped Hadley in the elevator. She'd held her shoulders with a firm, almost frightening grip. "Trojan horses come in many shapes and sizes," she said in a low, velvet-drape voice. "Beware of chocolate ones."

Hadley had nodded fiercely. "Chocolate Trojan horses. Gotcha. And hey—say bye to the gnomes for me."

Yup. Hadley sure did miss her old life. Invisible gnomes and all.

The idea of chocolate Trojan horses made Hadley suddenly regret leaving her lunch behind. Instead of the soy-butter sandwich, she envisioned a plate of chocolate chip cookies straight out of the oven, with the chocolate still warm and glistening.

Whenever she and her mother had an argument and both were too stubborn to apologize, her mother would sneak a few premade lumps of cookie dough into the toaster oven and then leave them on a platter for Hadley to find. It was her mother's way of saying she was sorry.

"I wish I had a plate of those cookies right now," she muttered, swinging her legs around the side of the bed. She shivered lightly. The house was always so cold.

Laughter crept in like a thief through the open window. It was Mom and Ed. Hadley's fingers drummed nervously on the mattress. The tiny voice inside her began niggling again.

Maybe I should take a peek. Just a peek to see what they're doing. Just to make sure they aren't having too much fun. Without me.

Hadley's bedroom window faced out the side of the house. She flattened her cheek against the cool glass and could see the driveway leading to the garage, which was detached from the main building. There was a room above it where a tenant lived. Some old lady Hadley hadn't yet met.

She lifted the wooden frame higher, stooped, and stuck her head out. Craning her neck as far as it would go, she still couldn't see the backyard. Then Hadley remembered the attic had two tiny octagonal-shaped windows. One that faced out the front of the house and one that faced the back. From either end, the house looked like a giant Cyclops. The back window was perfect. She could spy on the yard from it and remain unseen.

Hadley slipped out of her room and crept across the hall. Between her bedroom and Isaac's was what looked like a closet. The old hinges sang a chorus of complaints as she swung the door open, revealing a narrow flight of stairs. She stepped inside.

The air was thick and stale. It smelled of dirty socks and moldy cheese. Behind her, the door slammed shut. Hadley jumped.

"Drafty old house," she muttered to herself, and quickly climbed the steps.

The attic was small, made tighter by slanted walls. It hadn't been used for anything other than storage. Dust was thick as a rug and the cobwebs solid as curtains. Boxes containing books, candlesticks, and other ancient-looking things lay half draped in yellowing sheets. A rocking chair, a rusted lamp, and a broken tricycle were among the abandoned treasures.

Hadley sliced at the cobwebs with her bare arms as she waded through the clutter. Her eyes shot daggers in every direction, warning lurking spiders she would not give up without a fight. She made it to the far end of the room a bit grimy, but otherwise intact.

The window facing the back provided a perfect view of the garden. She leaned against the sill and peered out.

The sky was a lazy shade of summer. Fluffy white clouds hung in the air like ornaments on a tree. Below, the yard seemed to stretch on forever, dropping off into Hays Woods, which sprawled all the way to the Monongahela River. The canopy of trees was like a rolling green carpet. A light breeze fanned the weeds and wild grass Ed hadn't gotten around to mowing.

Hadley felt as though she were watching a secret silent movie. Isaac held the blue-and-orange kite above his head while Ed ran with the spindle. Ed was tall and gangly—like a daddy longlegs.

The string pulled tight and the kite caught the wind. It soared upward for a second, but Ed turned to watch it at the wrong moment and got tangled in his own legs. He performed a clownish pirouette before dropping to the ground. The kite dove, landing inches from his nose.

Isaac was laughing so hard he fell to the ground, too. Hadley's mother and Ed were laughing at Isaac. Everyone was having a great time. Everyone. Except Hadley.

That's when it hit her—she was the only Jackson in a house of Crenshaws. Why did her mother have to change her name when she married Ed? She'd never changed it when she'd married Hadley's real father, the father Hadley had never known.

Hadley let go of the sill and turned. She yelped as ice-cold fingers gripped her ankle and yanked.

Her legs came out from under her and her arms spread wide to cushion the fall. She landed with a huge *thunk* on her behind. A cloud of dust exploded from beneath her. She coughed and sputtered, waving at the air. Her ankle was caught in the spokes of the old tricycle.

"Weird," she muttered, pulling herself free from the steel trap. She could swear the tricycle had been clear on the other side of the room. She was certain she'd felt a hand. She reached to rub her ankle. That's when she saw it.

Her flailing hand must have snagged one of the old sheets,

because there on the floor, uncovered and glaring at her with its Cyclops eye, was a house. A dollhouse. An exact replica of the house she was living in.

Voices rushed up the stairwell. Hadley didn't want anyone to know she was spying. She got to her feet and rushed toward the steps, leaving the dollhouse exactly where she'd found it. Only when she glanced over her shoulder and took one last look, she couldn't escape the feeling *it* had found *her.*

Four

The fire in the woodstove has long since died. The room is dark and cold. I shiver, and then pull the wool cover over my head.

Papa has left early for the glasshouse. It is a good distance away along our property's edge. He works from well before dawn until long after dusk in the large barn. There they crush sandstone in large troughs and then smelt it in the opening in the enormous furnace to produce fine glass. I've seen the blazing furnace on a few occasions. It is a monstrous thing, reminiscent of a fiery dragon throat.

Papa employs twenty-one men and twelve boys. He calls them dog-boys, as they are trained to respond to the unique whistle of the men they assist. I tell him the name is disrespectful and unkind, and he tells me that is why he will not permit me to come to the glasshouse and upset things with

*my rebellious, visionary ideas. That, plus it is too danger-
ous. Papa says accidents can occur quickly.*

*Of course nothing could ever happen to Papa. He is an
expert glassmaker. He apprenticed at the prestigious Boston
& Sandwich Glass Company, where he then worked for
many years before leaving Massachusetts to begin his own
business in Pennsylvania.*

*Papa says he produces the finest flint glass in all of
Pittsburgh—perhaps in the entire Union. He is proud to
tell Mama and me that in the five years since he left us to
found Palmer Glass Works, it has come to rival even the
most exceptional of European imports.*

*I have only been in the city of Pittsburgh twice since my
arrival in Pennsylvania, but I wholeheartedly agree with
Mama—it is not nearly as lovely as Boston. Clouds of soot
billow from smokestacks. The dark, dense air hovers like a
gray blanket over the city, blocking out the sunshine during the day and the stars at night.*

*I lie in my bed thinking of Boston and my stately, be-
loved row house. All the while this new house creaks and
groans, and the wind wuthers in the chimney flue like a
strange symphony performed just for me.*

*Then, all at once, the symphony ends. The front door
creaks open, and dull footsteps clip-clop across the hall.
Frau Heinzelmann, the German woman Papa has em-
ployed to care for us, has arrived. She is a stout and sturdy*

woman, with a round face and rosy cheeks. A thick braid of nut-brown hair coils around her head like a snake.

I spring from bed, gather the wool blanket around my shoulders, and fly down the dark oak steps. Papa reminds me all the time not to charge like a buffalo down the steps or one day I will take a nasty tumble, but I do not heed his warning.

Papa has instructed Frau Heinzelmann to work silently so as not to disturb Mama, but as I approach the kitchen I can already hear her bustling about, clattering pans, singing cheerfully.

Der Jäger in dem grünen Wald,
muß suchen seinen Aufenthalt.
er ging im Wald wohl hin und her
ob auch nichts anzutreffen wär . . .

It is an old folk song she has taught me about a hunter in a green forest who meets a young girl with glowing eyes.

We must keep the house quiet for Mama. She has not adapted well to the change. She misses her sisters, Cordelia and Angeline. She longs for the streets of Boston, her favorite hat boutique, and of course the restaurants and cafés. Papa says Mama has a touch of melancholy caused by acute nostalgia. Frau Heinzelmann insists it is her spleen.

"Too much black bile brings on gloominess," says Frau Heinzelmann.

She has suggested a good leeching, but Papa is all for modern science—not what he calls medieval myths and peasant practices. Doctor Fenton has prescribed Mama a nerve powder and plenty of bed rest.

Today, Frau Heinzelmann has brought Mama a large clay pot brimming with wood violets. I stick my nose into the floppy blooms and inhale deeply. They smell sweet and mossy and wet-leaf green. It is like a whisper of summer entering our late fall lives.

I follow Frau Heinzelmann up the stairs into Mama's room. I hop onto her soft mattress. Mama turns and runs a hand down the long braids Frau Heinzelmann has given me. She smiles vaguely and says, "Hello, little bird."

Before I can respond, her eyes glaze, her hand falls limp at her side, and she is gone again. Today is a good day. Some days Mama does not speak at all.

"Sweet violets cure the soul," says Frau Heinzelmann, placing the plant on Mama's nightstand. She checks the porcelain chamber pot, but it is bone dry. "Mind, you can only smell them once. After that, the nose is deadened to the scent." She points to the rather bulbous feature in the center of her round face.

"I can still smell them," I tell her, sniffing the sugary aroma that has taken over Mama's room.

"Hush, child." Frau Heinzelmann ushers me out. "Go somewhere and play."

I heave a sigh. I would very much like to do just that, only I have no one to play with. Our neighbors are a great distance away, and Papa will not permit me to go off on my own. He does not want me to get lost in the woods. They lead to the Monongahela River.

Papa says Monongahela is an Algonquian word that means falling banks. Apparently the shoreline is unstable and quite treacherous. He worries for my safety. He believes if I get too close, I might slip in, and I cannot swim. He says the current would carry me to the Ohio River and then perhaps all the way to the Mississippi. He would never see me again.

Frau Heinzelmann claims it is not the current I should worry about but rather the strange man-fish known by locals as Monongy. She warns that the elusive aquatic beast will drag me under the waves should I so much as dip in a toe.

Of course, I do not wish to become Monongy's victim, so rather than venture outside or spend my days in solitude, I return to the kitchen with Frau Heinzelmann. While she cooks and cleans and irons the linens, she tells me old folktales of cunning toads and deep wells and lovely princesses. She sings songs about brave hunters and young maidens with bright, clear eyes.

Five

Hadley carefully maneuvered a pea with her fork from one end of her dinner plate to the other. Isaac wasn't allergic to legumes other than peanuts, so they ate peas almost every day. She was certain she was turning green.

"Why isn't *O* the first letter of the alphabet?" asked Isaac. He was famous for asking random questions designed to make Hadley ask *"What?"* She couldn't resist.

"What?"

"*O* is like zero. So it should be first, doncha think?" He shoved a spoonful of peas into his mouth, chomped a few times and then grinned. His teeth were covered in green mush.

Hadley rolled her eyes and sighed.

"I'm taking some time off next week," said Ed. "I'll paint the halls and the living room then."

"We picked Desert Dusk. Just like the old apartment, Haddy." Her mother beamed.

Hadley smiled and nodded. She was trying hard to be cheerful. When she'd left the attic that afternoon she'd discovered a plate of cookies—chocolate chip cookies with the chocolate still shiny—waiting at her door. It was a peace offering from her mother. Just like old times. Hadley had lifted the plate, but her pinkie finger seized and the cookies slid off, dropping to the floor in a heap of gooey crumbs. When she apologized for ruining the gift, her mother pretended she had no idea what Hadley was talking about.

"I almost forgot," said Ed. "My boss gave me three tickets to the Pirates game next week."

"Wow!" shouted Isaac. A pea torpedoed from his mouth, landing on the table in front of Hadley.

"Three?" said her mother, glancing at him nervously. "For you and the kids, of course."

People often spoke of the fifth wheel as being unnecessary, but Hadley was beginning to feel like the fourth wheel— on a tricycle.

"Of course," said Ed. "You like the Pirates, Haddy, don't you? Isaac and I are huge fans."

"Pirates? Sure." Hadley smiled weakly. "I like football."

Isaac burst out laughing. "The Bucs are baseball, silly."

"Bucs?"

"Bucs. As in *buccaneers*," said Isaac. "As in pirates."

"Looks like you have a lot to learn about sports," said Ed, tousling Hadley's hair.

"Sports. Great." Hadley smoothed her hair and took a deep breath. Her mind drifted toward the dollhouse.

Of course she hadn't played with dolls in years, but this was different. The dollhouse fascinated her. Everything was identical to her new house. The tiled roof, the octagonal windows high in the attic—it even sat on a wooden base complete with a driveway, artificial grass, and a garage set back with a room above it. It was as though someone had taken her house and shrunk it.

Hadley had once visited a strange museum in Niagara Falls. It was full of all sorts of weird miniature exhibits. There was a pair of shoes that had belonged to the tiniest woman that had ever lived, plus a bunch of shrunken heads—supposedly real heads—that had had their skulls removed and then been sewn back up and stewed in herbs by the Shuar people of the Amazonian lowlands. There was even an entire woman shrunk to the size of a doll—though Hadley had read later that it had been a fake, most likely created using goatskin.

Questions mushroomed in the darkest regions of her brain. Whose dollhouse was it? Who built it? And why had its owner left it behind?

The idea of dolls suddenly reminded Hadley of the eye. Her hand swam into her pocket but came out empty. It must have slipped out when she'd fallen in the attic. She resolved to search for it later.

"Pass the biscuits," said Isaac.

Hadley handed him the basket of warm buckwheat blobs. Her pinkie finger was still stiff. Another casualty of the fall.

Ed crammed a slab of meat into his mouth and talked while he chewed. "We'll stay in motels and eat at greasy diners. I've saved up vacation and my boss says I can use it all next summer."

The words *next* and *summer* snapped Hadley's attention back to the dinner conversation. She struggled to catch up. "What are you guys talking about?"

Her mother looked at Hadley as if she had three heads. "I'm sure I told you. We're going to take a family vacation next summer. A road trip south."

Hadley's chest tightened. Her fork fell, sending a glob of mashed potatoes splatting onto the table. "You promised I could go to Camp Greenly Lake with Sydney next summer. Remember?"

"I said maybe." Her mother swiped at the mess with her napkin, only making it worse. "But things have changed."

Hadley felt the last grain of her old life slip through her grasp. The thought of going to camp with Sydney next summer was what had made leaving her best friend bearable.

After the dishes were cleared, Mom, Ed, and Isaac decided to play a board game. Hadley leaned against the door frame.

"Come on, Haddy," said Ed. "We can be teams. You and me?"

He patted the seat beside him. The skin around his eyes crinkled when he smiled. He was trying so hard to be nice. Hadley really wanted to take him up on his offer, but when she opened her mouth what came out was, "Some other time."

Isaac rolled the die and drew a card. He had to act out a word while Hadley's mother and Ed had to guess. He danced around while they shouted random things like "Potato!" and "Sherpa!"

Beyond their voices, Hadley heard something else—a low wispy wail, like the sound of a child crying. It was coming from the enormous fireplace in the living room.

The oak mantel stretched floor to ceiling. It was covered in elaborate carvings. With the empty timber basket sitting there, it reminded Hadley of a great grinning mouth. Wind whispered down the long shaft, echoing out the brick firebox.

The timer buzzed.

"Goggles," said Hadley softly. "Isaac's word was 'goggles.'"

"Of course," said Ed, putting his arm around Hadley's mother and winking. "It was so obvious."

Her mother seemed to really enjoy the game. She and

Hadley only ever played things like chess and checkers and gin. Most games didn't work well when there were only two players.

It was funny how Mom and Ed had met. Hadley's mother was a parking enforcement officer. Ed was a painter. One day, he had to make a quick stop at one of his work sites and couldn't find parking. She'd given him a ticket for parking illegally. He thought she was so beautiful that he double-parked in the exact same spot every day for the next three weeks, hoping to see her again. He got about a dozen tickets before she returned to that block. He said he would have gotten a million tickets if that was what it took to find Hadley's mother again.

They'd barely started dating when they'd decided to get married. They hadn't introduced Isaac to Hadley until they were already planning the wedding. It all happened so fast; a license, a bunch of daisies, dinner at a fancy restaurant, and it was a done deal. There wasn't even time to blink.

"Sometimes," her mother had said, "you just know it's right."

Hadley wondered what had made things so right with Ed and so wrong with her real father—so wrong that Hadley had never even been allowed to meet him. So wrong her mother kept no pictures of him at all. Whenever she'd asked her mother what he was like, her mother always said the same thing: *He's not a very nice person. Let's leave it at that.*

Hadley went to bed early. She lay awake for hours, teetering on the brink of sleep. Now and then a low groan rippled through the walls. Her mother said old houses were like old people—they had tired, creaky bones.

She tossed and turned, trying to get comfortable, but her mind overflowed with wild thoughts she couldn't tame. Thoughts about Sydney making a new best friend. About strange dollhouses, and tricycles that moved on their own. About ice-cold hands clawing her ankles. And one-eyed dolls.

Hadley had just drifted off when something startled her awake. She sat bolt upright. In the slit of space between the floor and her bedroom door, a shadow skittered past her room.

Six

Hadley sprang from her bed and flung open the door. An enormous full moon hung suspended in the sky. It bathed the landing in a silvery glow. The scrap of darkness was gone.

"A rat," she hissed. What else could it be?

Hadley wasn't afraid of rats. She'd made peace with city creatures that skulked out of the sewers after dark. But sewer-dwellers were one thing—houseguests were a different story. If the house was infested with diseased vermin, she might be able to convince Mom to leave and return to their old apartment. And their old life.

She searched the length of the baseboards looking for an opening, and her eyes settled on the slit beneath the narrow door. The attic. She was suddenly certain that was where the rat had gone. She would search the attic, find the nest, and be packing her bags by morning.

As she crept down the hall, her body cast a long, lean shadow on the opposite wall. It was distorted, alien-like.

She arrived at the narrow door and paused before swinging it open. She was worried the old hinges would sound the alarm and wake the entire house. Luckily, Ed's snoring could drown a jet engine. She gripped the knob and pulled quickly between Ed's *ahhh* and *guurrl.*

The air was cool and damp. Faint shuffling sounds drifted down from the floor above. The rat must be foraging through the boxes of junk. Carefully, she climbed the steps.

Reaching the attic, Hadley was suddenly angry for not having thought to bring a device to record the evidence. Who would believe her without proof?

Pale moonlight filtered through the octagonal windows, illuminating the cramped space. Careful not to startle the creature, Hadley peered in and around the boxes.

When she found no sign of rodent activity, she pushed the boxes this way and that, desperate to locate the intruder. She practically tore the place apart, no longer caring who she woke, but could find not a single tuft of furry evidence.

Frustrated, she was about to leave when her gaze settled on an object glowing in the moonlight. Lying on the floor, in plain view, was the eye.

Hadley picked it up. It glistened like an icy pearl. On the floor in front of her sat the dollhouse. It seemed to her the eye and the house belonged together. Hadley knelt and peered inside.

In the room above the garage, she saw furniture—a floral sofa, a miniature coffee table, and a bed at the opposite end near the kitchenette. And lying on the bed was a doll—a wooden doll, like a marionette but without strings.

The doll had snow-white hair knotted into a bun. It wore a white blouse with ruffled sleeves and a pale lavender skirt. The eyes were large and glassy—too large for its delicate face.

Hadley held the eye beside the doll. It was the right size, only this doll wasn't missing an eye.

Inside the main building there were three other dolls—a man, a woman, and a little girl. She hadn't noticed any of them earlier that day, but then she hadn't had time to investigate the inside of the house.

The mother doll sat opposite the father doll on the sofa in the living room. The little girl lay on her bed in the room that was now Hadley's. The old woman looked like she could be the girl's grandmother. Not one of the dolls was missing an eye.

The father doll wore brown pants and a plaid shirt. Hadley smoothed his hair and adjusted his glasses.

Hadley had never met her real father. She didn't know the first thing about him. Ed seemed like a good enough guy. He was great with Isaac. And he was trying hard to be friendly to Hadley. But, somehow, it just wasn't the same.

Hadley lifted the little girl doll and puffed up her pink frilly dress. This girl was lucky, thought Hadley. She had the perfect family. Hadley wished her family were like these dolls. The room went cold and a shiver snaked up her spine.

Someone's walked across your grave, her mother would have said. It was a silly saying. An old wives' tale. Hadley placed the doll back on its bed. The house was drafty. And she was exhausted. That was all.

Hadley heaved the house into her arms. No matter whom it had belonged to before, it was hers now. Swaying under its weight, she maneuvered her way down the narrow flight of steps and into her room.

She placed the dollhouse gently on the floor between her bed and the window. Then she took the eye from her pocket, placed it on her nightstand, and crawled back into bed.

The numbness had traveled from her pinky finger into her palm. But when she reached over to massage away the pins and needles, she sliced through thin air. Her hand had disappeared.

Seven

Whatcha doing?"

Isaac thumped toward Hadley's bed like a puppy whose feet had outgrown him. He stuck his face an inch from hers and grinned. Morning sunlight sparkled through the sheers, setting his rust-colored freckles on fire.

"Sleeping," she grumbled.

Between searching for the rat and imagining that her hand had somehow evaporated, she'd gotten little rest. Such a strange thing—one moment, she could have sworn her hand was gone. And then, just like that, it was back again.

His eyebrows stitched together. "If you're sleeping, how come you're talking? And how come your eyes are open?"

Hadley sat up, forcing Isaac back.

"What's that?" he asked, pointing to her nightstand.

"Nothing," she said, snatching the eye and closing her fingers tightly around it. "Quit being so nosy."

"What does fear smell like?"

Hadley flopped back onto her bed. *What?*

"People say dogs can smell fear, so I was wondering what fear smelled like."

"I don't know," said Hadley. "I guess it smells sour. Like sweat."

"Hey! Cool!" he shouted, diving for the dollhouse. "Where'd you get this?"

Hadley scrambled out of bed. "In the attic. Leave it alone."

Before she could stop him, Isaac grabbed the man doll. "Let's play!" He made the doll fly through the air like a superhero. Hadley snatched it out of his hands.

"I. Don't. Play. With. Dolls." She pronounced each word slowly and clearly so there was no confusion. She set the man back in the family room on the sofa across from the mother.

Isaac shrugged. "I do. I wanna play with it."

"I've told you a thousand times not to come in here and mess with my stuff." She was about to usher him out of her room when Mom called.

"Breakfast!" she hollered. She didn't need to call twice.

Isaac raced down the stairs, practically tripping over himself to get there first. Hadley took her time, throwing on a pair of shorts and a T-shirt. She pocketed her eye, and arrived in the kitchen with Isaac already elbow-deep in a bowl of cereal.

"Flaxy O's!" he shouted, like they were the greatest things ever invented.

Hadley dropped into a chair in front of a bowl overflowing with dirt-colored rings covered in flax seeds.

While Isaac munched loudly, Hadley contemplated whether or not she should tell her mother about the rat infestation. She decided without evidence her mother would think she was making it up. The Flaxy O's stared at her, looking annoyingly superior.

"Weren't you going to make egg-free rice-flour pancakes?" Hadley asked. Her mother had taken a few weeks off work to move and get settled. Hadley was hoping the free time would translate into some fancy breakfasts.

"Not today," said her mother. "I promised Ed I'd get a start on clearing out the garage. You're going to help me, aren't you?" It wasn't a question.

Hadley shrugged. She could think of a thousand things she'd like to do with her mother—cleaning the garage was not one of them.

She pulled her bowl toward her and poured cold milk over the muddy-looking O's. Each spoonful tasted like sawdust. She had to stop several times to pick seeds out of her teeth.

"Can I help, too?" asked Isaac, sputtering bits of cereal and milk over the table.

Hadley cast her mother a frantic look. *Can't it be the two of us? Just this once? Please.*

Her mother turned toward Isaac and smiled. "Of course. We can use all the help we can get, can't we?"

We. Hadley used to like that word. Only *we* no longer meant her and her mother. *We* now meant Hadley, her mother, Ed, and Isaac. Hadley was developing a *we* aversion.

The doorbell rang.

"I'll get it," said Hadley, happy to escape *we* for the moment.

The dark wooden door was swollen with August humidity. Hadley gave it a hard tug and it flew open. She narrowed her eyes. "Hey."

"Hey."

It was Gabe. He held out a cinnamon-scented slab on a purple plastic plate. "My grandma made an extra date-and-nut loaf."

He swiped at his floppy hair. It drooped back over his eyes. He'd come by a few times, and already he'd decided he was Hadley's new best friend. She was going to have to set him straight.

"Isaac's really allergic to nuts. We can't even have any in

the house." She eyed the lopsided lump of a loaf, desperate for a taste of something flax-free.

"Sorry," said Mom, appearing in the hallway. "Tell your grandmother thanks anyway."

"We're going to clean the garage," said Isaac, pushing past Hadley. "Wanna help?"

Hadley sighed. Apparently *we* now included Gabe. *We* might as well include the entire northern hemisphere.

"Can't right now," said Gabe. "I'm breeding *Amphimallon solstitialis.*"

Hadley frowned.

"That's European June beetle to you laymen," he added.

Hadley would have reminded Gabe it was August, but she already knew better than to encourage him. Long-legged, slimy, and slithering things were all he talked about. No wonder he spent a lot of time in the woods—alone. He wanted to be an entomologist. Or anthropologist. Or archaeologist. Some kind of ologist.

"Well, have fun then . . ." Hadley was about to close the door when he held out his hand.

"I'll come by later," he announced, as though he were doing her a huge favor.

Before Hadley could protest, Mom and Isaac accepted his offer. Gabe nodded and left with his loaf, practically bouncing down the porch steps.

Hadley shut the door and stomped back to the kitchen. She'd barely had time to sit down to her now-soggy bowl of Flaxy O's when the doorbell rang a second time.

"I'll get it," she huffed.

Hadley yanked at the sticky wooden door again. "What *now* . . . ?" she began, but her voice shriveled and slid back down her throat. It wasn't Gabe.

A woman with dark glasses and silver-white hair stood on the porch. She wore a white blouse and a faded lavender skirt. She had a round face and rosy cheeks.

"Hadley," she said. "I'm glad we finally meet." She smiled a broad, satisfied smile.

"Hello, Ms. de Mone," said Hadley's mother, who had come to the door. "Won't you come in?"

"No, no," said the old woman. "I just stopped by to bring you this. I nearly stumbled on it while doing my morning walk." She held out a newspaper rolled up with a rubber band.

"Sorry about that," said Hadley's mother. "The driveway's long and the paperboy's lazy. I'll tell him he's got to bring it to the front door from now on."

As she took the newspaper, Hadley's eyes snagged briefly on the headline. Bold black letters announced: *MISSING*

"Are you sure you don't want to come in for a bit?" asked

Hadley's mother. "The house is a disaster, but you're more than welcome to join us for breakfast."

"Thank you." She smiled. "But I've already eaten." She extended a hand toward Hadley. "I live in the room above the garage. I'm Althea S. de Mone. But you can call me Granny."

Eight

Papa has brought me the loveliest gift!

It is a dollhouse identical to our new home. One of his glassblowers—who had previously apprenticed with a woodworker—has crafted it. It has such exquisite detail and, of course, real glass windows! Papa has even included the carriage house, above which Frau Heinzelmann lives.

Naturally, I brought my dolls, Emmaline and Alexandra, with me from Boston, but Papa says he will have another surprise for me shortly, and I am delighted, for I suspect it will be a new doll.

Though Papa still feels somewhat like a stranger—after all, I only saw him twice in the five years before Mama and I joined him—he is truly working hard to win my affection.

I place the dollhouse in the parlor beside the fireplace, where I can keep warm as I play. When it gets chilly, I lift a heavy iron poker and prod the burning logs. Sparks burst upward in a dazzling display. The smoldering logs warm my hands and face.

A whisper of snow already covers the fields, and the bitter November winds moan down the hollow throat of the chimney. Sometimes, when I am alone, I imagine I hear voices. They call my name.

"The house creaks and groans," I tell Frau Heinzelmann. "It frightens me."

She beats a ball of dough on the wooden table. She is making dark rye bread, which Papa insists has the taste and texture of a shoe sole.

"That is only the kobold," she puffs. "Pay it no mind."

Papa does not want me spending my days with Frau Heinzelmann. He has purchased several books for me to study, including a brand-new novel by the acclaimed author Herman Melville. It is titled Moby-Dick and tells the story of a crazed Captain Ahab and a great White Whale. It is quite interesting, but I tire of reading all day, and since Papa has yet to find me a suitable tutor—and with Mama lying ill in bed—Frau Heinzelmann continues to be my only company.

"The kobold?" I ask, wrinkling my nose at the unfamiliar word.

"Why, the house spirit, of course. Every home has one."

She slams down the dough. A cloud of flour puffs into the air around her.

My hand flies to my mouth. "A spirit? There is a ghost in the house?"

I stare horrified at the empty air around me, but Frau Heinzelmann goes about her bread-making business, seemingly indifferent to my concern. She waves her sausage-like fingers dismissively.

"A kobold is a little sprite. A kind of goblin. Have I not told you the story of the shoemaker and his elves? Or of Rumpelstiltskin, that nasty little fellow?" She swipes a floured hand across her forehead, leaving a dusty trail.

I shake my head.

"Once upon a time, there lived a poor shoemaker and his wife . . ."

I sit and listen, spellbound, as she recounts the entire tale of the kind elves that help the poor shoemaker and his wife until the wife makes them a set of clothes and they disappear forever. She goes on to tell the tale of the crafty imp-like creature Rumpelstiltskin, who helps a young maiden spin straw into gold.

I sit transfixed, my entire body hanging on her every word. All the while she kneads her dough until it is round and smooth. When she is finished, she drops the ball into a greased pan and sets it aside to rise.

"We are lucky," she says. "A kobold is good to have. They help with chores. Sometimes, I am sure ours has folded the linens, for when I attend to the task, I find it has been done." She nods and winks knowingly.

Frau Heinzelmann picks up a bucket filled with soapy water and hands me a rag. She swipes the excess flour from the table with her large hands. When she is done, I run the rag over the surface, rubbing hard to clear any trace of sticky dough. Papa would be displeased to see me doing servant work, but I like to help.

"Where were you born?" I ask her, as she tosses the flour into the sink and claps her hands. She washes them with some of the soapy water.

"In Oberlahnstein—a small town on the banks of the Rhine River." She does not look back at me, but her head rises and she stops moving, and I can tell she is picturing the place.

"Do you miss it?" I ask.

Frau Heinzelmann turns and smiles. "I do," she says. "The rivers here are lovely, but they are quite different from the Rhine. Many old castles and ruins sit perched high on its banks. I miss the cobblestoned streets, the many festivals, and, of course, the bakeries. Yes. I miss the bakeries a great deal." She pats her belly.

"Do you wish to return?" I ask, suddenly sad for her as much as for myself.

She pauses as if to think. "No," she says at last, but more softly than I am used to her speaking. "Pennsylvania is my home now." She reaches out and wiggles my nose, leaving a spot of dampness on the tip. "And it is yours now as well."

"Tell me another story," I ask eagerly. "With elves and goblins and pretty maidens."

Frau Heinzelmann smiles. "First we finish cleaning the kitchen, or the kobold will be upset. They do not like untidy homes. And they can become quite nasty little creatures if you cross them."

Nine

It rained unexpectedly that afternoon. Sheets of warm water draped to the ground, drenching the lawns, sending muddy rivulets gushing along both sides of the street.

Without sunlight, the white walls of Hadley's bedroom were gray and gloomy. She crouched in front of the dollhouse and picked up the doll that looked like Althea S. de Mone. She studied it closely. Its clothes were similar to the old woman's. So was its hair.

Rain trampled louder on the rooftop as lightning streaked across the sky. A loud clap of thunder shook the ceiling and walls. Isaac burst into her room.

"Granny's really nice!"

"Stop barging into my room!" Hadley's heart beat through her words. She placed the doll in the house. "Can't you at least knock?"

"Knock, knock."

"*What?*"

"Knock, knock," he repeated. "You say, 'Who's there?'"

Hadley rolled her eyes and sighed. "Who's there?"

"Althea."

"Althea who?"

"Althea tomorrow!"

Isaac threw himself on her bed, erupting in giggles before she had a chance to react. "Althea—*I'll see ya*—get it?"

A smile muscled its way through Hadley's frown.

"Hey," he continued. "What do you think her middle name is? It starts with an S."

Hadley sighed. "No idea."

"How about Someday—Althea Someday! Or Saturday—Althea Saturday!" He continued to laugh hysterically.

Taking Isaac by the arm, Hadley escorted him to the door. "Very funny. Now can you please leave?"

"All right, all right." He yanked his arm free and strolled into the hallway. He poked his head back into the room. "Althea later!" He ducked back out and laughed loudly all the way down the stairs.

Hadley lifted the girl doll. She looked about the same age as Isaac. She had curly brown hair tied back with a bright pink ribbon that matched her pink dress. Her eyes were soft and brown. Like Hadley's. She set the doll back on her bed.

Drops of rain wove zigzag paths down her bedroom window. Something Isaac had said kept echoing in her mind: *Granny's really nice.*

Hadley had never had a grandmother. She imagined what it would be like to have someone spoil her rotten. Someone who would invite her for sleepovers and bake all sorts of treats like cookies and crumbles. Together, they would watch old movies and play pinochle, collect worthless coins, and knit scarves so long only giraffes could wear them.

She pressed her cheek against the cool glass and peered toward the garage. Dark drapes hung heavy in Althea's window. A word tripped on her tongue and stumbled out of her mouth. "Granny."

It rained the rest of the afternoon and on into the evening. The only good thing about the nasty weather was that it kept Hadley from having to clear out the garage. It also kept Gabe from pestering her.

After dinner, Hadley helped her mother clean up in the kitchen. When she finished drying the dishes, she lowered the rag. She made a tight fist with her left hand and then slowly relaxed it.

"What's wrong?"

"I'm not sure," Hadley said. She flexed her fingers and rubbed her palm. It still felt so strange and tingly—like it didn't belong to her anymore.

"Did you bump it?" Mom took Hadley's hand and examined it.

"I fell yesterday. Nothing serious." She didn't want to tell her mother she'd been spying on them from the attic window.

"Well, let me know if it doesn't get better, and I'll make a doctor's appointment."

Hadley nodded. It felt good to have her mother focused on her for a change.

"Where did you find that dollhouse?"

"In the attic."

"Looks like an antique. Could be worth a lot of money," said her mother. "Take good care of it. They don't make toys like that anymore."

Hadley considered the possibility. The house was well over a hundred years old. "There's a doll that looks like Ms. de Mone."

Her mother laughed. "Really?"

"It's even wearing the same clothes as her. Well, similar. Don't you think that's odd?"

"Why don't you ask Ms. de Mone the next time you see her? She really likes you. She told me so."

Hadley smiled. Maybe she could get used to having a granny after all.

That night, Hadley went to bed early. The dull day had

made her tired. She got into her purple penguin pajamas and switched off the light. She was about to pull her blinds shut when she stopped. She stared at the dark drapes hanging in the window above the garage. She wondered what Althea de Mone was doing.

"Probably sleeping," she told herself. "Old people go to bed very early."

When she turned to get into bed, she glanced at the doll-house. Something had changed. The family of dolls was sitting at the kitchen table. Althea de Mone's doll was no longer on its bed where she'd left it. It was propped against the window over the garage. Staring at her.

Ten

Isaac refused to admit to sneaking into Hadley's room and playing with the dolls. He was always messing with her stuff, moving things around, borrowing things—even after she'd told him a thousand times to stay away. She'd never had to share anything before. It was still a new concept for her.

To keep Isaac away from her things, Hadley helped him fly his kite. She tried to play catch with him, but she wasn't very good. Instead they played badminton and croquet with rusty equipment they found in a box behind a recycling bin in the garage.

Gabe came over every morning. With nothing better to do, Hadley joined him. Together they explored the upper edge of the ravine, and even wandered into the woods along the intertwining trails. Despite his intense love of creepy-crawlies, he was beginning to grow on her.

"What's that?" he asked.

Hadley stood at the edge of her yard, holding the eye up to the sun. Light shone through it, casting lacy patterns on the grass. "An eye." She tucked it back into her pocket.

"Where'd you find it?" he asked excitedly. "Did you excavate it?"

"Actually, *it* sort of found *me*," she responded vaguely. "In the house."

His expression collapsed. Clearly he was expecting a more exciting response. He focused his attention on a worm that had strayed onto a rock.

"Did you know, in terms of sheer number, insects are the most dominant life form on Earth?"

"Nope."

"Actually, they appeared over four hundred million years before humans."

"Marvelous," said Hadley. "So, er, how long have you lived here?" she asked, swatting at a fly. There seemed to be an extraordinary number of flies near the edge of the ravine.

Gabe picked up the worm, dug a small hole, and placed it inside. He pushed soil over the top, patting it gently so as not to harm the worm. "On the earth?"

Hadley rolled her eyes. "In your house."

"All my life," he said. "I was born in my house."

"I was born in a hospital," said Isaac, swooping in behind them, diving headfirst into the conversation.

"He didn't mean he was actually born in the house, silly," said Hadley.

Isaac watched Gabe's every move, trying to imitate him. Except that Isaac dug up a worm first in order to rebury it, which sort of defeated the whole rescue purpose.

"I *was* born in my house," said Gabe. He found another insect in distress—a beetle being attacked by ants. He dusted off the scavengers and set the creature on its way. "In the living room, to be precise. My mother's never had a great sense of timing. She's kind of spatially challenged, too. One time"—he chuckled—"she tried to fit a whole pineapple into a blender. And then she forgot the lid and . . ."

A sunset flushed across his cheeks as he explained in great detail the disastrous results of the un-lidded blender episode.

"So, where are your parents anyway?" Hadley asked, trying hard to sound casual.

"They travel a lot. For work."

"Really? What do they do?"

"Mom is a nuclear engineer," said Gabe. "Dad's a long-haul trucker."

"Wow," said Hadley, eyeing Gabe with newfound respect. "So, what do they have in common?"

"Fuel."

Gabe then subjected Hadley to several more bug stories seriously lacking plots. She listened quietly and even reluctantly helped with his experiments.

First, they placed half a teaspoon of sugar near an anthill and timed how long it took for the ants to notice. Next, they placed some honey on a tree trunk to see what sort of insect would be attracted first. Hadley hoped for a butterfly. But all they got were tons of flies. And more ants.

As the days passed, Hadley kept a watchful eye on the room above the garage, hoping to steal a glimpse of Althea S. de Mone. One day, Hadley nearly went right up to her door and knocked, but her mother stopped her. She said not to pester Ms. de Mone—she was old and needed plenty of peace and quiet.

"She knew my name," said Hadley one morning at breakfast.

"What's that?" her mother asked, pouring yet another bowl of Flaxy O's.

Hadley sighed. Aside from tasting like wood chips, the cereal had a horrible effect on her digestive system.

"She said she knew her name," echoed Isaac. He grinned at Hadley before shoveling a truckload of cereal into his mouth. He chewed loudly. Just like Ed. Hadley decided it must be genetic.

"Who knew whose name?" asked her mother. She was distracted by her kitchen cleanup and didn't appear to be following the conversation too closely.

"Ms. de Mone," said Hadley. "The day she came, she called me by my name before you introduced me."

"She heard me say it when I came to the door."

"But you didn't."

Her mother frowned. She stopped scouring the sink and stared at the ceiling as though replaying the scene in her mind. She waved a dismissive hand in the air like she was swatting a fly.

"I told her about you before that morning, Haddy. I told her all about you when we first met, the day Ed and I brought her the documents to sign the lease."

"But . . ." said Hadley, "how did she know it was *me*? She can't see, can she?"

"She's not blind," said Hadley's mother. "She's only visually impaired. Bright lights bother her. Now stop imagining things. She's a lovely lady. The perfect tenant. She's even invited you for afternoon tea. She said something about having baked a crumble . . ."

Eleven

One of Hadley's Flaxy O's went down the wrong way. She choked and sputtered. "She's invited me for *what*?"

"I love crumble!" shouted Isaac. "What kind? Peach? Blueberry? Do you think she has any dairy-free whipped topping?"

Her mother's smile quivered. "I'm sorry, Isaac. She's only invited Hadley. It's probably not wheat-free or nut-free anyway. It wouldn't be safe for you."

Isaac nodded sadly as the crumble rug was yanked out from under him. A twinge of guilt tugged at Hadley's insides, but part of her was secretly delighted to be a *she* and not a *we* for a change. Plus, Hadley was excited to ask Ms. de Mone about the dollhouse.

"What time?" she asked.

"After lunch." Her mother narrowed her eyes. "Be polite. And don't overstay your welcome."

The morning hours bled into one another like a wet watercolor. Before long it was lunchtime. Gabe was over again, asking if Hadley wanted to go into the woods with him—he was hunting for snakes. He seemed truly disappointed when she told him she had other plans.

At quarter past one, Hadley stepped out into the warm glow of the afternoon. Across the street, two neighbors stood in front of a flower bed. A little girl was trying to do a cartwheel on the lawn. They all stopped and waved in unison when they saw Hadley. She fanned her fingers half-heartedly. She'd gotten used to the tingly feeling in her hand, not to mention the overly friendly neighbors.

She'd made it halfway to the garage when the screen door of the apartment flew open and Althea de Mone appeared. In one hand, she held a casserole dish. The other hand waved eagerly. "Right on time!" she announced.

A soft breeze carried the tasty aroma of baked apples, cinnamon, and brown sugar straight to Hadley's nose. Her legs moved independently of her brain, and before she knew it she'd climbed the cast-iron steps and was standing in the doorway. The delicious scent filled the apartment, drawing her inward.

"Come in, come in," said Althea de Mone, smiling at Hadley over her shoulder as she led the way inside. "It isn't often I have the pleasure of guests."

Hadley's eyes adjusted to the dim light. She gave the

room a quick scan. There was a floral sofa on one side with a coffee table in front of it. A bed lay opposite the kitchenette. They were identical to the three pieces of furniture in the dollhouse.

To the left of the kitchenette sat an old wooden trunk—the kind you might find packed with blankets, extra sheets, or towels. Althea set the casserole on the low table in front of the sofa and directed Hadley toward it.

"Smells delicious," she said, sinking into the squishy cushions.

"Make yourself comfortable. I'll get the tea."

On either side of the dish sat two powder-pink plates and two dainty silver forks. Althea de Mone retrieved two matching pink teacups and two saucers and placed them beside the plates. She returned to the kitchenette and then sailed back with a silver teapot and a bowl filled with a pale yellow sauce, half custard, half cream.

When all was set and ready, she placed a heaping spoonful of crumble on Hadley's plate and a smaller portion on her own. To each she added a dollop of the thick, rich cream. Then she carefully poured the tea, and a musky aroma mingled with the apples and cinnamon.

"I hope you like it," she said. "It's an old recipe."

Hadley lifted a forkful of crumble to her mouth. It was sweet and nutty and practically melted on her tongue. Maybe it was all the Flaxy O's she'd been eating, but Hadley swore she'd never tasted anything quite so delicious. She quickly ate another forkful and another. Althea de Mone smiled enthusiastically. Hadley smiled back. She could see her own reflection in Althea de Mone's glasses.

"Do you have to wear those all the time?" she asked.

"Too much light hurts my eyes. I can't see at all if it's too bright."

"I'm sorry . . . ," said Hadley uncomfortably.

"Oh, don't be sorry, dear. It's my retinas—afraid my cones are defective. But my rods work quite well. They're what allow you to see in the dark. That's why I keep the apartment dim."

Hadley didn't know a thing about cones or rods, but she thought it must be horrible not to be able to see well. While she ate, she couldn't help but examine the old woman further.

Her skin was like an apple left too long in the sun, but between the creases there was a smoothness that made Hadley think Althea de Mone must have been really beautiful when she was young. There was something cozy about her, too, like an old silk pillow.

Hadley had barely finished her last mouthful before Althea began spooning another portion onto her plate. "This is great," she said between mouthfuls. "What's in it?"

"The apples are the secret. They're from the root cellar. The house keeps them fresh and crisp."

Hadley's mother had said something about there being a lot of food in the root cellar, but Hadley didn't think it was still edible. It was kind of strange eating food someone else had left behind. She stared suspiciously at the crumble remaining on her plate.

"There, now," Althea de Mone said. "Isn't this pleasant?"

Hadley nodded.

"Try the tea."

Hadley picked up the dainty cup and took a tiny sip. It tasted like cranberries. And nutmeg and cloves. "Tasty," she said. "Reminds me of autumn."

For a few minutes neither spoke. But it didn't feel awkward—it felt like they'd known each other forever.

Hadley took a few more sips of tea. She set her cup down gently. "Ms. de Mone," she began.

"Granny. Please."

Hadley paused, worried the word wouldn't come out right. But this time it slid easily off her tongue. "*Granny* . . . How long have you lived here?"

She rubbed her wrinkled hands, her expression thoughtful. "Quite a long time."

It was exactly what Hadley wanted to hear. "You obviously knew the previous owners?"

Althea sat back and sighed. "The house has had many owners." She picked up her teacup. "So many people have come and gone. I'm afraid I'm losing track." She took a sip. "I guess I'm just lucky no one has evicted me yet."

"Do you know there's a dollhouse that looks exactly like our house?"

"You found it?" she said cheerfully.

Hadley nodded. "In the attic. Do you know anything about it? Who made it?"

"Well," she began, "I've heard tell the original owner of this house moved here from Boston. He had the house built especially for his wife—he wanted her to be happy in her new home. The dollhouse was a gift to his daughter. His only child."

Hadley's mother had been right. The dollhouse was an antique. Possibly worth a lot of money.

"There's a doll that looks like you," Hadley said.

Althea chuckled. "That old thing?" She took Hadley's empty dish and walked toward the kitchen. "I made it myself. Do you really think it looks like me?" She held up her chin, then turned her head to the right and the left, flashing Hadley her profile from various angles.

The mystery was solved. "Exactly like you. But wasn't it hard to make, what with your eyesight and all?"

She patted Hadley's head. "As I said, dear, my rods are fine. I see quite well if the light's not too bright."

They chatted for some time about all sorts of things—the town, the woods, the neighbors, and the weather. Hadley told

Ms. de Mone all about her old apartment, about her worries on starting a new school, and about how much she missed Sydney.

Finally, Hadley stood and stretched. "I'd best get going."

She stepped toward the drawn drapes. She wanted to know if she could see her bedroom from the window. She was about to open them when she remembered Althea de Mone's light sensitivity.

"So soon?" said Ms. de Mone.

"I told Mom I wouldn't overstay my welcome."

"All right." She chuckled. "But promise you'll drop by again soon?"

"Sure," said Hadley, secretly hoping it would be for more crumble. She picked up her teacup and saucer and set them in the kitchen sink.

"In fact," continued Granny, "why don't you drop by to-morrow? Late afternoon. They should be ready by then."

Hadley stopped at the door. "They?"

"Run along, now," said Althea de Mone, shooing her out the door. "I don't want to spoil the surprise."

Hadley's mouth stretched into a wide grin. Having a grand-mother was just as she'd imagined. A fuzzy feeling filled her insides as she descended the steps. She hurried down the driveway and into the side door.

Perhaps it was the crumble, but that night Hadley went

to her room with the warm feeling still lingering in her stomach. She had a grandmother—at least a substitute—and it felt good. It even made her feel better about sharing her mother with Ed and Isaac.

She was about to turn out her light and settle into bed when she glanced at the dollhouse. Althea de Mone's doll lay in the room above the garage. The other three dolls were missing.

Twelve

Papa surprised me yesterday with another gift. It was, as I expected, a doll. But not any ordinary sort of doll—this one looks exactly like me!

It has long blond braids and wears a pretty pink dress quite similar to the one Aunt Cordelia has sent me from Boston. The round cheeks and sharp nose carved into the pale wood are mine—even the lower lip juts out a little too far, just as Frau Heinzelmann claims mine does. But the most incredible of all the doll's features are its eyes.

Papa made them himself. He told me that he began with a white glass tube and a torch. He held the tube over the flame until the glass was soft enough to separate just the right amount. Holding the piece over the flame, he blew gently to create a bubble.

He holds his finger up and blows on it to demonstrate.

Next, he says, he heated a rod of pale blue glass and inserted a glob to form the perfect iris. To this, he joined layers of silver and gray twisted canes for depth and sparkle and to give the iris a lifelike color and quality.

He points to his pale gray eyes, which are identical to mine. I gaze deeply into them and see the silver folds he is talking about. Then he makes a silly face, startling me. I laugh out loud and he laughs as well. Once we catch our breath, he continues.

Using a narrow dense black rod, he tells me how he fixed the pupil. He says this was the most difficult task. If he did not get the pupil exactly in the center, my doll would appear cross-eyed. He crosses his eyes and puffs out his cheeks. We both burst into giggles.

When Papa leaves for the glasshouse the next morning, I examine the large sparkling eyes—almost too large for the dainty little face. They seem so real—so lifelike—I'm certain they follow my every move. Unfortunately, the doll is far too large for the dollhouse, but Papa says he will have some smaller dolls made soon.

"What does a kobold look like?" I ask Frau Heinzelmann, setting my doll on the kitchen table in front of me.

"Why, whatever it fancies, of course."

Frau Heinzelmann pounds slices of pork into thin, tender pieces. Each time her wooden mallet descends, the whole kitchen shakes. "It can appear as a cat or a marten. A child. Or even a candle's flame."

My doll hops with each assault of the mallet, but I catch her before she topples to the ground. I run a finger along her braids. "And where does it live?"

Frau Heinzelmann dips the pork pieces into a bowl with raw egg and then drags them across a plate of bread crumbs, which stick to the cutlets.

"Under the threshold of doors, beneath old steps, behind the stove, or in the fireplace . . ."

"I want to see it," I say, eagerly eyeing the shadowy corners of the room.

Frau Heinzelmann melts a slab of lard in a large cast-iron skillet. She will fry the breaded pork into crisp schnitzel. After that she will make an apple strudel using apples kept crisp in our root cellar.

There are many pickles and preserves in the cellar as well. Frau Heinzelmann has prepared them all in lovely glass jars Papa made especially for her. Papa is getting used to her cooking, which he claims has added inches to his waist.

We bring Mama's food to her room, but even when she feels well enough to eat she only nibbles a bite here and there. Mama has grown so pale and gaunt, Papa and I worry terribly for her health.

"Kobolds do not like to be seen," Frau Heinzelmann

says, tossing a cutlet into the sizzling lard. The meat hisses and snaps, the lard frothing up on its sides. "But if you catch one, it might do as you please. Perhaps tidy your room for you. Or polish your shoes. Or grant you a wish."

I sit up straighter. I would very much like a little creature to do my bidding. I would wish it to play with me and sing songs to me and keep me company.

"I'm going to catch it," I tell her with a fierce resolution.

Frau Heinzelmann smiles at first, but then her smile turns to a frown. She wags a finger heavily crusted with crumbs. "Mind you, don't anger it. I warned you, they can be malicious little demons, those kobolds, if they become angry." She plunks a basket filled with potatoes in front of me. "Now, until you have a kobold to do your bidding, peel!" she orders. I pick up the paring knife and reluctantly oblige.

That night, I sit in the parlor near the fireplace pretending to play with my dollhouse. Frau Heinzelmann has retired to her room above the carriage house for the evening.

Mama lies in bed sleeping, and Papa is in the dining room eating a late supper. I listen to the whispering in the chimney and I think. And I am curious.

Before I left the kitchen that morning, I sneaked a fistful of bread crumbs into my pocket. I withdraw them now and make a neat line leading out of the fireplace toward where I sit. I wait and watch for the longest time, but nothing stirs.

Papa calls to me and tells me it is late and I should be in bed. Reluctantly, I agree to go to my room, but before I do I have a thought. I want to catch the kobold. I want to see it. So I sneak back into the kitchen and locate a pot of molasses.

Without Papa seeing, I pour some of the thick, sticky syrup onto the floor where the line of bread crumbs ends. Then I place my dollhouse in front of the mess so Papa won't see. I join him in the dining room to bid him good night.

"Good night, little bird," he says, having adopted Mama's pet name for me. "May your dreams be sweet wishes, and may your wishes come true."

I glance over my shoulder at the line of bread crumbs leading to my dollhouse. I nod at Papa and smile.

Thirteen

Grace!" shouted Hadley.

A woman at the edge of the lawn stood dappled in morning light. She had a carpetbag purse slung over one shoulder and held an enormous bouquet of sunflowers as tall as herself. Muddy roots tangled around her long white skirt, leaving brown stains.

"I came to say hi," she yelled, "and to cleanse the house's aura for you."

Hadley and her mother exchanged grins.

"Who's that lady with the purple hair?" asked Isaac, joining them. "And why is she standing in the street yelling at you?"

"That's Grace," said Hadley. "She's our friend from the old building. Don't worry, she's just a bit kooky."

Hadley was so happy to see Grace that she forgot she was mad at Isaac for hiding the dolls. She charged down the steps of the porch and across the lawn.

Layers upon layers of beads of all shapes, colors, and sizes swung from Grace's neck. Purple Birkenstock sandals that had seen better days covered feet that Hadley was sure had never entered a spa. Grace's hair was a ball of magenta frizz, and her eyes bulged behind cheap rhinestone-rimmed frames with no lenses.

Hadley took Grace by the hand and dragged her toward the house. They reached the front porch and climbed the steps. Grace handed Hadley's mother the sunflowers and clapped the dirt from her hands. She dusted her skirt, which only made the stains worse.

She looked Hadley up and down. "Your feet have grown." She looked at Isaac. "You have a loose tooth. Only it hasn't started wobbling yet." She patted his shoulder.

Isaac's fingers shot to his mouth and began checking his teeth one by one. "I think I found it!"

Hadley's mother smiled. "Thanks for the flowers." She held them at arm's length so as not to get dirt all over herself. "Come in. I'll show you the place. Just, er, let me get a vase for this lovely bouquet."

Grace looked at Hadley and shrugged. "They're not really from me. The gnomes picked them."

She was about to step inside when she came to a dead stop in the center of the door frame.

"It's worse than I thought," she muttered, peering inside the house. "We'll need the full treatment. A thorough aura scrubbing, spirit exfoliation, atmospheric renewal, and buffing. And some thalassotherapy, too. Good thing I brought my algae, seaweed, and alluvial mud kit." She patted her large purse and winked knowingly.

Hadley sighed happily. She was glad Grace had come.

Hadley's mother boiled a pot of hot water—it was all Grace drank—and then they sat down in the living room for a chat.

Grace told them all about the other apartment residents. Mostly random details, like how Mr. Barolo had thrown out a perfectly good chair and that was why he now had a horrible case of gout, and how Evelyn and her twins had started a hunter-gatherer diet except they ate far too much bacon which stank up the entire fifth floor upsetting Alfred who was a strict vegan.

She was particularly annoyed with the mysterious young couple that had moved into Hadley's old apartment. Apparently they refused to take the elevator. Or say hi to the gnomes.

The old apartment. Just the mention of it made Hadley homesick.

While Grace talked, Hadley reached into her pocket, turning the eye over and over between her fingers. She recalled details of her old bedroom. The inside closet door where her mother had etched her height each year. The stain in the carpet where Sydney had dropped the jar of grape jelly. Her puce walls—which she could never properly describe. Were they purplish brown? Grayish violet? How she missed her puce walls.

Hadley's mother went to the kitchen to boil a second pot of water. Isaac, who had lost interest in Grace, wandered up to his room.

"I wish my walls were—" said Hadley, but Grace dove across the sofa and clapped a hand to Hadley's mouth, muffling her last word.

"Never make wishes," she gasped. "They can be granted."

Hadley peeled Grace's fingers from her mouth and smiled. "But—isn't that a good thing?"

"Of course not." Grace removed her glasses and wiped the nonexistent lenses on her skirt. She then placed them back over her eyes and her expression brightened as though she could suddenly see a whole lot better.

"The universe is a giant cosmic seesaw. We tip to the left, then to the right. Up and then down." She swung her body side to side, up and down for effect.

Hadley swayed with her, nodding feebly. The cosmic seesaw was nauseating.

"And there's a rhythm, too. Like waves hitting the shore. Like the moon affecting the tides. Like planets rotating around the sun. What goes out comes in. What goes around comes around. Whatever you send forth comes back. So if you get something, you must give something in return. Do you understand?"

"Not really," said Hadley.

She closed her eyes to let her stomach settle from the cosmic roller-coaster ride. She wondered if there was a remedy for cosmic motion sickness hiding in Grace's bag.

They drank several cups of hot water, ate a few biscuits, and then took Grace on a tour of the house.

She pulled out a yellow feather duster and waved it in each room, muttering to herself in a language Hadley was certain was gibberish. Grace stayed for another quick cup of hot water, then said it was time for her to head back to the gnomes. She gave Hadley a huge hug, promising she'd be back soon.

"Drop by and visit whenever you like. The gnomes have been asking for you."

Hadley stood at the front door watching until Grace was a colorful blur at the end of the street. Ed's car rolled into the driveway just as the tingling creeping up Hadley's left arm made it all the way to her elbow.

"Hey!" he shouted, stepping out of the car. "I took the afternoon off, and guess what?"

"Dad!" said Isaac, pushing past Hadley. He ran down the steps so quickly he nearly stumbled, but caught his balance in the last moment. Ed gave him a swing-around hug.

"I need your help, buddy," he said, walking to the trunk.

He opened it and pulled out two buckets of paint. He handed them to Isaac, who sagged under the weight, and told him to take them to Hadley's mother.

"Desert Dusk!" She beamed so brightly Hadley thought she might need Granny's sunglasses to look at her. "Can we get started today?"

"Nope," said Ed, pulling a third bucket from the trunk. "I've got another project I need to do first."

He walked toward the porch and stopped right in front of Hadley. He held out the can, a goofy grin on his face. "Didn't you say you wanted your room painted?"

Hadley stared at the can. The label had only one word.

Puce.

Fourteen

There are five."

"Five," said Hadley, nodding. "That's a lot." She stood at the edge of the ravine, gazing out into the woods.

"Possibly six," said Gabe. "And the strange thing is, they weren't there yesterday."

"How can you be sure?"

"Because I checked." Gabe scanned the ground with massive binoculars that had probably belonged to his great-grandfather. "There was only one nest yesterday. Today, there are six."

"They must be migrating," she told him.

Gabe shook his head. "Snakes don't migrate. Their habitat doesn't change, so there's no reason for migration."

Hadley's eyes swept the murky brush. The ground was spangled with last year's leaves. Rocks jutted out from the clay-like soil, and roots tangled above the surface in lacy patterns.

"What about winter? Do they hibernate?"

"No," he scoffed. "Snakes don't hibernate either. They go deep into their holes and spend the winter there inactive."

Hadley rolled her eyes. "Sounds a lot like hibernation to me." She kept an eye on her feet in case any snakes decided to slink up unexpectedly.

Gabe let the antique binoculars drop. They thudded against his chest and he winced. "You don't know much about snakes, do you?"

"Nope," she said. "Don't want to either."

"Well, I know a lot about them, and what I can tell you is there was one nest yesterday and there are six today."

He glanced to the right, then to the left. He leaned in close and looked her straight in the eye, whispering as if someone might hear.

"There are more insects, too. Tons of flesh flies. And I saw a centipede the length of my hand and a beetle the size of a doughnut." He picked up his binoculars and fixed them on a spot in the ravine not twenty feet down and pointed. "There."

Hadley followed his gaze. Snakes were bad enough, but monstrous multi-legged insects were a whole other horror. She cringed.

"It's like"—Gabe swung around—"something is drawing them to this spot . . ."

Hadley stared through the lenses that made Gabe look an awful lot like a giant bug himself. "Hey, Gabe," she said suddenly, "do you think the universe is in perfect balance?"

Gabe dropped his binoculars. They slammed against his chest a second time. "Well," he began, "the sun's gravitational forces push in, while its nuclear forces push out and . . ."

Hadley sighed. "No, no, no. I mean, do you think everything has to balance out?"

He ignored her. "Of course, there's Newton's third law—'For every action, there is an equal and opposite reaction.' That's balance, too."

Hadley couldn't let on she had no idea what he was saying. "Right. Newton's third law. You know, I always confuse it with his eighth."

Gabe frowned. "Newton doesn't have an eighth law."

Hadley's cheeks flushed. "Of course he does."

"No. I'm sure there are only three."

"He wrote five more later on," Hadley lied. "Maybe you just didn't get past the first three."

Gabe folded his arms across his chest and raised his chin. "So, what exactly is Newton's eighth law?"

Hadley picked at some dirt in her fingernail. "I can't remember it exactly, but it's something like, 'For every fig that goes into a cookie, there is an equal and opposite amount of dough required.'"

"You made that up," he said.

"Did not," she insisted. "Haven't you heard of Fig Newton cookies? Why do you think they named them after him?"

Gabe squared his shoulders and opened his mouth. Luckily Isaac dove in to save her.

"Hey!" he called, scampering toward them. "Whatcha doing?"

"Going snake hunting," grumbled Gabe.

"*You* are going snake hunting," Hadley corrected, jabbing a finger into his shoulder. "*I* am going inside."

"Suit yourself," he shrugged. "But you might miss some pretty interesting stuff."

"That's a chance I'm willing to take," shouted Hadley, as Gabe slid into the gully.

"I wanna go!" said Isaac. "Can I?"

Hadley hesitated. "I'm not sure. It's dangerous down there. You could get lost. I think you should ask—"

Before she could finish her sentence, Isaac was scrambling down the slope into the trees, after Gabe. "Hey! Wait up!"

"Come back!" called Hadley, but he ignored her.

She tried a few more times, but Isaac disappeared into the brush. He was probably safe with Gabe. Still, Hadley decided she'd best let her mother know what he was up to. She turned to walk back toward the house, stopping when she reached the garage.

Granny de Mone had told her to come by late afternoon. Hadley was so excited and so curious, for a moment she forgot all about Isaac.

Climbing the metal steps, she opened the screen door and rapped once, lightly, on the wooden door. It creaked open. She must have knocked harder than she'd thought.

Granny stood at the far end of the apartment with her back to Hadley. "Come in," she said gently. "They're ready."

"What's ready?" The faint aroma of apples and cinnamon lingered in the air. Hadley could live off crumble if she had to.

"Your gift," said Granny de Mone, turning.

In her arms, she held something. Hadley squinted, but she couldn't quite make out what it was. She took a few steps closer. Light from the open door cast a pale iridescent beam on the objects. Granny was holding three wooden dolls. A man, a woman, and a little boy.

She placed the dolls into Hadley's hands, one by one, beginning with the doll that looked like Hadley's mother.

"This looks like Mom," Hadley said, examining the doll with hair combed back in a tidy ponytail just like her mother's. It wore a pretty cotton floral dress. Her mother rarely wore dresses. When she wasn't in uniform, she just wore sweats.

The second doll looked like Ed. It had gangly legs and wore a T-shirt and jeans—just like Ed. The third had sun-burned freckles—a shade only Isaac's skin could achieve.

"Wow," she said. "They're amazing."

Granny smiled. "Really? Do you like them?"

"Yes! I do! How did you make them?"

"I carve them. I'm sort of an amateur sculptor. Helps me pass the evenings when the light is easier on my eyes." She pointed to her glasses. "Plus I can feel the faces as they take shape." She ran a finger along Ed's doll's nose.

"Cool."

Hadley turned the dolls over in her hands. She couldn't get over how beautiful they were.

"There's one of you, too," said Granny. "Only it's not quite ready."

Hadley beamed. She could really get used to having a grandmother.

"Be careful, though," said Granny. "They're a bit fragile."

Hadley nodded and her grip on the dolls tightened. She was about to ask if Granny could show her how to make them when she heard a *thunk*. It came from somewhere inside the apartment. She searched the room, but didn't see anything out of place. Althea de Mone didn't seem to notice.

Poor Granny, thought Hadley. *Her hearing is as bad as her eyesight. Getting old must be awful.*

"Run along, now," Granny said. "Have fun playing."

Hadley smiled and nodded. She left the apartment and hurried down the steps. She could hear Gabe whistling in the ravine. Her smile quickly faded. She couldn't let Gabe see her. She didn't want him to think she still played with dolls. She made a beeline for the house.

She raced through the front door and dashed up the steps to her bedroom. She was moving so fast she missed the final step and stumbled. Her hand flew out to grab the railing, and one doll slipped from her grasp. It thumped down step after step until it lay at the bottom of the staircase.

That's when she heard the scream.

Fifteen

Ed came rushing out from Hadley's bedroom. His T-shirt and jeans were covered in brown-violet splotches. Hadley nearly thought it was blood, but then she remembered her puce paint.

"Are you okay?" he shouted.

"It wasn't me," she said frantically, though the scream had sounded like a young girl, and had echoed in the hallway all around her.

She and Ed stood staring at each other for a moment, frozen in shock and confusion. Then they heard a second, shriller cry. This time it distinctly came from outside.

Hadley set the dolls on the landing. She and Ed raced to the bottom of the stairs, where her mother almost crashed into them. They all exchanged frantic looks as a third scream split the silence. They scrambled out the door.

Gabe was carrying Isaac across the yard toward the house. He was calling for help while Isaac was crying and holding his leg.

"It's his ankle!" shouted Gabe. "I think he broke it!"

Ed rushed over and took Isaac in his arms. He tried to calm him with soothing words.

"Keys!" shouted Hadley's mother.

Hadley hurried back to the house while Ed and her mother ran toward the driveway. Gabe jogged alongside her.

"I'm really sorry," he said. "He followed me into the ravine."

They were in the car in a flash. Hadley leaped into the back seat beside Isaac, who stretched out his leg. He leaned his head on her shoulder, sobbing. She placed her arm around him and squeezed his hand while Ed tried to comfort him. They drove off, leaving Gabe standing on the lawn looking distraught.

They made it to the doctor's office in record time. Thankfully he said it was only a sprain, though a pretty bad one. Isaac was going to need to wear a plastic cast until the swelling went down.

When they arrived home, two of the dolls were sitting on the last step. Hadley scooped them in her arms. In all the commotion, she couldn't recall having set them there. The third doll was still sprawled facedown on the floor where it had fallen. She picked it up and smoothed its hair. It was Isaac's doll.

"Where did you get those?" asked her mother.

"Granny made them for me."

Her mother took the Isaac doll and examined it. "They're lovely. Such detail. Must have taken her a lot of time. You should write her a thank-you note."

"Mine's the coolest," said Isaac, grabbing it. Ed carried him up the stairs toward his bedroom. "I'm going to name him Little Isaac. Can I keep him in my room?"

"No," said Hadley. She snatched the doll from Isaac's hands. She'd promised Granny she would take good care of the dolls. Isaac's had already taken a tumble. She didn't want anything else happening to it.

Hadley's mother frowned. "I want to talk to you," she said. "Privately. Wait for me in your room."

Hadley lay on her bed in her half-puce room, propped on her elbows, staring at the dolls. She took the eye from her pocket and held it beside each of the faces. It might have belonged to any one of them—only these dolls weren't missing eyes.

The door creaked open and Hadley sat up. Her mother entered, shut the door, walked calmly toward the bed, and sat down on the edge. Before Hadley had a chance to say a word, her mother blasted her.

"What were you thinking? How could you let Isaac go into the woods without telling me? He's only six years old. Those trails are like a maze. He could have gotten lost and ended up clear over by Glass Run Road. Or at the creek. Or worse at the river and—oh, I don't even want to think about it!"

Her words stung. She was right, of course, but couldn't her mother see how terrible Hadley already felt? Shouldn't she be trying to make Hadley feel better, not worse? She wanted to apologize, but before she could, a second round of accusations exploded.

"You should have kept an eye on him. Honestly, sometimes you can be so irresponsible."

Hadley's jaw quivered. Her cheeks grew hot. Her mother had never spoken to her like this in the past. She wasn't even giving Hadley a chance to explain how Isaac had run off before she could stop him. She clutched the eye tightly, pressing it so hard against her palm she was sure it would make a permanent dent.

"You should have taken care of him. He's your little brother."

Tears pooled in Hadley's eyes. Her mother's words stabbed the air between them. "He's *not* my brother."

Her mother stood and walked toward the door. "I'm tired of your selfish, sulky behavior," she said. "Until you're ready to apologize and start acting like one of the family, you might as well stay here." She left the room and closed the door behind her.

Hadley felt as though she'd been slapped across the face. Her mother hadn't even given her time to explain. She hadn't even tried to hear Hadley's side of the story.

Her anger spiraled out of control. Hadley glared at the dolls that looked like Ed and Isaac. "I wish you'd never come into my life," she hissed.

A gust of icy air blew into the room. She left the bed to shut the window. As she tugged at the sticky wooden frame she felt the blood crackle through the veins in her right hand. She made a tight fist and then released it, stretching her fingers to their limits. The hand felt heavy and hollow—just like her left hand.

Hadley stayed in her room the rest of the evening. She got ready for bed alone. It took her forever to fall asleep. She tossed and turned, burrowing deep into her feathery duvet.

She awoke with a start when her bedroom door opened and then shut.

Still hazy with sleep, she stood and lunged for the door. Who could have snuck into her room? And why?

"Isaac," she whispered suddenly. He must have come looking for his doll, Little Isaac. He was going to take it and hide it like he'd taken all the other dolls. But this time, she would foil his plan.

With her duvet wrapped around her shoulders, Hadley flew into the hallway. Isaac couldn't walk quickly with the cast on. His door was wide open. She dashed toward it and poked her head inside.

"Isaac!" she whispered.

There was no answer.

"Stop pretending you're asleep. I know it was you!"

She searched his room, but the darkness was playing tricks on her. She fumbled for the light switch and a zillion dots swarmed her eyes. Slowly, they adjusted to the bright light, but once they did, her vision narrowed to a fine point. Her knees buckled and her head hit the floor with a tremendous *thwack*.

Sixteen

I awake in the middle of the night. I have had strange dreams and I am certain I hear noises. Sharp nails clawing on wood. Scritch. Scratch. Scritch. *It grates at my ears.*

Papa will not allow me to keep a kerosene lamp, as he worries it may tip and cause a fire. Instead, on my nightstand I have a brass saucer with a stub of a candle. I slip out of bed and strike a match. My ceiling and walls explode into wicked shadows.

The sound grows louder. Scritch. Scratch.

There are many wild animals in the woods behind our house. I worry a raccoon or a skunk—or worse yet, a black bear—has gotten into the house. I decide I must wake Papa.

My nightshirt flutters around my feet as I tiptoe into the hall. The candle flame ripples outward, pressing into the thick darkness. I take a step toward Mama and Papa's room, but I stop quite suddenly. A thought awakens in my mind. I turn toward the stairs and slowly descend.

My bare feet are cold as I glide along the wooden floors toward the parlor. I stand for a moment at the threshold, staring at the grand fireplace mantel. Embers of last evening's fire still glow hot. They cast a reddish glow onto my dollhouse.

Scritch. Scratch.

I take a few tentative steps until I reach the side of the dollhouse. My gaze follows the trail of now-missing crumbs that once led from the fireplace to the molasses spill. I expect to find some poor little shrew or helpless vole caught in the sticky syrup, but as my eyes settle on the spot, the breath catches in my throat.

My hands tremble, and it is all I can do to keep the candle from slipping from my grasp. For a moment, I wonder if perhaps I am dreaming, if perhaps I am wandering in my sleep, if this is some sort of fata morgana—a mirage, a figment of my dream-drenched imagination. I blink hard, but it does not disappear.

On the floor, covered in sweet black syrup, is a human-like form no larger than one of my dolls. It twists and turns, clawing violently at the floor with the fear and fierceness of an injured animal. It is a mass of tangled hair and seems unable to free itself from the sticky molasses. Though the very idea of this peculiar creature terrifies me, it seems at once both small and helpless, and I am quite suddenly sorry for what I have done.

I set the candle in front of the house and fly toward the kitchen, where Frau Heinzelmann keeps her bucket filled with soapy water. I return as quickly as possible and pour the contents on top of the creature's head, soaking it from tip to toe. The syrup dilutes, and dark liquid spreads into a larger but less sticky stain.

The creature frees itself, and I get a better sense of its figure. It has thin alabaster limbs with razor-like claws. Long white hair flows down from its head, concealing its body. Its face is angular, with cheekbones so sharp and jut-ting they could slice bread. It glares at me with enormous dark eyes—so black I almost think they are two giant holes.

I take a step back. I am ill prepared for such a hideous sight. I had imagined a kobold to be a charming and chubby little pixie wearing peasant clothes and a red felt hat— nothing like this gruesome ghoul.

I take another step backward. I turn to flee, but it calls to me in a calm but commanding voice.

"What have you done? Why have you caught me? What is it you wish from me?"

More than ever, I know I should run fast to my bed and

pull the covers over my head, but something holds me steady. *Frau Heinzelmann's words come back to me. If you catch one, it will do as you please . . .*

I muster all my courage and turn slowly to face the creature. "I wish," I begin tentatively. Then I take a deep breath and forge ahead. "I wish you to do my bidding."

The creature's eyes appear to grow larger and darker still, and I suddenly want to withdraw my words. Before I am able, the creature responds.

"What is it you desire?"

Frau Heinzelmann was right! It is magic and can grant my wishes! Thoughts travel through my mind at a tremendous speed, and before I truly know what I am doing, words are tumbling out of my mouth.

"I would very much like my papa to be home and not to spend all his hours in the glasshouse!"

The creature smiles, and beyond its thin lips I see it has sharp little teeth.

"And I would like Mama to be up and out of bed. I would also like to return to Boston . . . and I would like a companion—yes—someone to talk to and play with and stay with me always . . . and . . ."

"You ask a great deal," interrupts the little creature suddenly. Its eyes are so large I fear I could fall inside them and be lost forever. "However, if you promise to give me something in return—*if you swear it*—then you shall have all you desire."

Hurray! I shall have my wishes! And though a warning thuds softly inside me, I lick my dry lips and make a cross over my heart.

"I promise," I vow solemnly.

No sooner have the words left my lips than the creature vanishes. The candle flame extinguishes, leaving me sitting alone in cold darkness.

Seventeen

Sunlight melted into Hadley's room, forming puddles of gold on the ground.

She was sprawled across her bed, knotted up in her duvet. She unraveled herself, yawned, and stretched. Her body was as stiff as an old piece of licorice.

She'd had the strangest dream. It was gone now, snuffed out by the morning light, the last scraps fading fast into the soupy darkness of her mind. All that lingered was a slightly uneasy feeling. She sat up and ran her fingers through her tangled hair.

The door creaked open.

"Wake up, sleepyhead," whispered her mother. "Rise and shine." She stood in the doorway, swathed in a hazy glow. Her voice was fuzzy-slipper soft.

Hadley rubbed her eyes to get a clearer look, but her mother had already left the room.

"Breakfast is ready," she called cheerfully over her shoulder. "I've made your favorite."

Hadley's heart ballooned. Her mother must have felt awful about the previous night's argument. She must have thought things over and, instead of a plate of warm cookies, she'd made Hadley's favorite breakfast—caramel-peach French toast with whipped cream. Hadley could already taste the warm peaches. Even made with rice bread, fake eggs, and whipped topping, it would still be a treat.

She swung her legs over the side of the bed and stood. Her legs were wobbly, like she was walking on them for the first time. She made it halfway down the stairs when her thoughts were snatched by the delicious scent of cinnamon and brown sugar. She was dragged down the rest of the steps and into the kitchen.

Her mother stood near the stove. She carried a dish of sugary awesomeness toward the table. She wore her best pants, a white blouse, and a necklace with little dangling pearls.

"You're the best," said Hadley, plunking herself into a seat. The table was set with two plates, and there was a can of whipped cream already waiting. "I'm really sorry about last night."

"Last night?" said her mother vaguely. She placed three pieces of French toast onto Hadley's plate. She dug up extra peaches and caramel sauce from the casserole dish and piled them on top.

"You know," said Hadley, with downcast eyes. She really did feel awful about their argument.

Her mother shook the can of whipped cream vigorously and sprayed an enormous tower of white fluff onto Hadley's already full plate. "No. I don't."

Hadley picked up the can and examined it. Real whipped cream. "I didn't mean to behave so badly," she said. "It's just—"

"You never behave badly," interrupted her mother.

Hadley chuckled, certain her mother was being sarcastic. But then she saw the blank look on her face.

Her mother reached over and stroked Hadley's hair. "You're the best child a parent could ever hope for. You mean everything to me."

Ever since Ed and Isaac had come into the picture, Hadley had felt cast aside—like an outgrown pair of shoes. She had longed to hear her mother tell her how much she loved her. How much she meant to her. But as Hadley sat there listening to these very words, they seemed somehow strange. Unnatural.

"Is this peanut-free, wheat-free, and egg-free?" she asked, placing a forkful into her mouth. "Because it sure doesn't seem like it. And what's the deal with the real whipped cream? It's not dairy-free."

"You're such a character," said her mother. She grinned, as though Hadley had just said something funny. "Oh, and I thought we'd do each other's nails after breakfast. Would you like that?"

"Sure!" said Hadley. She could hardly believe it. First, her favorite breakfast. And now a girls' spa day. She decided her mother must really have been feeling terrible about their argument as well.

"With tiny jewels. Just like you like it."

Hadley smiled and nodded. She ate a few more bites of the tasty breakfast. Then suddenly her mother began stomping her feet. It startled Hadley and she jumped.

"Go on," said her mother. "Guess!"

"What?"

"The song. Guess the song."

The game. Her mother was playing their game. Only this time Hadley had to guess. They hadn't played in so long, Hadley had nearly forgotten how much fun it was. She tried hard to figure out the tune. She guessed several times unsuccessfully. The song had an awkward rhythm, one she was almost certain she'd never heard before.

"I don't know," she said finally, gulping her last few bites. "What is it?"

"It's the 'I Love Hadley' song. I just made it up this very instant!" Her mother grabbed the can of whipped cream, shook it hard, and poured another huge cloud of creamy white onto Hadley's plate, still stomping her feet loudly.

Hadley stared at the oozing mound and frowned. "I think I've had enough."

Her mother stopped stomping. "Okay. We'll save the rest of the can for tomorrow. I'm going to make your favorite again."

Again? thought Hadley. Her mother never made sugary breakfasts more than once a month. And what with all Isaac's allergies, it was more like never.

"Where's Isaac?" she asked. The smell of the breakfast should have brought him running.

"Isaac?"

"Isaac. My stepbrother. Ed's son. The kid who lives with us. That Isaac." She chuckled.

Her mother wasn't laughing. Or even smiling. She just stared at Hadley with a glazed expression. A deep chill settled into Hadley's bones, and her mouth went dry.

"Where's Isaac?" she said, more urgently.

"Stop teasing, Hadley," said her mother. "You know we live alone. Just the two of us. Exactly the way you like it."

Hadley's last bite of food threatened to rise back up her throat. "W-what did you say? What's going on? Where are Ed and Isaac?"

"I don't know any Ed. Or Isaac for that matter," said her mother. "Am I supposed to?"

Hadley gripped her mother's hand. She searched her

eyes long and hard, hoping to find a shred of something—anything—that might tell Hadley she was playing a cruel trick. Her eyes remained steady, vacant. Her smile, unwavering.

Reality was like a thin piece of paper folding in around Hadley. She kept hoping her mother would shout "Gotcha!" Or maybe Ed and Isaac would pop out from somewhere and yell "Surprise!"

Her gaze darted nervously from her mother to the puddle of melting whipped cream, around the kitchen, and into the hallway. She must be dreaming. There was no other explanation. She remembered waking in the middle of the night. She recalled her door opening and closing and then . . .

Hadley leaped to her feet. She charged out of the kitchen and raced up the steps, practically diving headfirst across the landing and into Isaac's room. She crashed into its emptiness.

Isaac was gone. Nothing of him remained. Hadley's heart exploded in her chest. She stepped backward, shaking her head, and then darted out into the hall and to her mother's room.

She searched everywhere for any sign of Ed, but there was nothing. No sign of him whatsoever. Not one single shred that indicated he had ever been there. Desperate, she yanked at the drawers one after another, but all his sweatshirts and jeans and sports jerseys were gone. Every stitch of his clothing. Everything. Gone.

Hadley took a deep breath. This couldn't be happening, she told herself. She raced into her bedroom.

The dollhouse glowed in the morning light. Hadley's mother's doll stood in the kitchen. Granny de Mone's doll lay peaceful and still in the room above the garage. But the Ed and Isaac dolls had vanished.

Hadley barely made it to her bed before her knees gave out. She lay for the longest time, thinking, rubbing her numb hands. It was as though someone had wrinkled the fabric of reality, changing the pattern of its threads. She closed her eyes. Perhaps if she dozed off, she'd wake from the nightmare and things would be back to normal.

Her mother came to check on her. She asked if Hadley wanted anything more to eat. Or if she wanted to go shopping for brand-new clothes. Her mother said Hadley could buy whatever she wanted. Then she located a brush and began brushing Hadley's hair.

"I'm going to get dressed and go outside," said Hadley, nudging her mother. She had to get away to think.

"Fresh air is good for you. I want you to be healthy, of course. Your health and happiness are all that matter." She began picking strands of Hadley's hair out of the brush. "Shall I come with you?"

"No," said Hadley, pushing her gently away. "I'd rather go alone."

"Of course. Whatever you say. I've got to finish painting your room anyway." She pointed to the half-puce walls. "I'm sorry I didn't get it done for you yesterday."

Hadley watched as her mother laid out the strands of her hair in a neat row on the bed. "What are you doing?"

Her mother smiled. "You know, silly. My special hobby." She held up her arm.

Hadley took a closer look at the bracelet around her mother's wrist. It was a tight coil of braided human hair. Her gaze then traveled to the necklace her mother wore. It was also made from braided hair. And dangling from it weren't pearls. They were Hadley's baby teeth.

Eighteen

Puce, **often misspelled** as *P-U-S-E* or *P-E-U-S-E,* is French for flea," said Gabe. "A bedbug is a kind of flea.

"Are you even listening to a word I'm saying?"

Hadley sat on a giant rock that jutted out over the ravine. She held the eye in her hand, turning it over and over between her tingling fingers.

Gabe was hoisting up an old log. He wore a yellow plastic hard hat with a light, like he was some kind of miner. He was looking for slaters—commonly known as pill bugs—and which he happily informed Hadley were, in fact, crustaceans.

"Anyway, my walls are now puce," she said. "And not because I asked for them to be—because at first I thought I might have—but now I'm sure I didn't. They're puce because I wished it. And there's more—"

"The color puce is not actually named after the insect, but the rust-colored stains left on bed linens after the bedbug has been squashed."

Hadley waved her hands in frustration. "That's disgusting! And totally irrelevant!" She sighed and leaned back onto the rock. "Gabe. Listen to me. Please."

Gabe stopped. He looked at Hadley, his headlight glaring in her eyes. He let the log fall, turned off the light, and joined her on the rock.

Other than the buzzing flies, the woods were quiet. Hadley inhaled the fresh scent of the wild plants and mossy trees.

A billion questions torpedoed through her mind—and Gabe was the first person she could aim them at. Did he remember Ed and Isaac? What did he think happened to them? Where did they go? Did he believe wishes could be granted? If so, how? Did he think she was crazy?

A chorus of birds chirped loudly.

"Gabe, I . . ."

"They're attracted to the insects." He pointed to the trees. "All those birds."

Hadley nodded. "Great. Listen, Gabe . . ."

"It's not time for them to migrate, so I couldn't figure out why so many are gathered, but I think it's the insects. The flies," he continued.

Hadley sighed. Gabe was now a bird expert as well.

"The insects attract birds and rodents. The birds and rodents attract snakes. It's like a strange micro ecosystem just beyond your house. Only I can't figure out what the flesh flies are attracted to. They usually lay their eggs in rotting flesh. That, or dung."

"Gabe!" Hadley shouted. "Will you listen to me? Ed and Isaac—my stepdad and stepbrother. Do you remember them?"

The tiniest of glimmers lit in the far depths of Gabe's green eyes, and for a moment Hadley was sure he remembered. Then his expression clouded over and his thoughts seemed to drift backward, disappearing into themselves. "Who?"

Tears prickled at the backs of Hadley's eyes. "Please, Gabe. Try and remember. Isaac? The boy who sprained his ankle? You carried him up the ravine?"

Any spark of recognition had been extinguished. Gabe shrugged and shook his head.

Hadley dropped the eye. She let her head fall into her hands. How could this be happening? Was she losing her mind? She glanced over her shoulder. The house's Cyclops eye was staring at her.

"Gabe—who lived in the house before me?"

He thought about it for a moment. "Well . . . the main

house was empty for quite a while, but I've heard things. Rumors."

Hadley grabbed him by the shoulders. "What kind of rumors?"

"Well . . . like . . . the family who lived here before you . . . one day—they were just gone."

Hadley nodded. She knew that. They had abandoned the place. That's what the realtor had said. That was why the bank had sold the house and her mother and Ed had gotten it so cheap.

"Some say they couldn't pay their mortgage so they up and left. Others say . . . they kind of . . . *disappeared.*"

"Disappeared? As in *poof*?"

He nodded.

She looked down at the glass eye lying in the dirt. She picked it up and carefully cleaned it off. "Poof," she repeated.

"Everyone says the house is haunted. That's why people keep abandoning it. They leave the furniture—even the food in the cupboards."

"Haunted?" Hadley gulped. "Why didn't you tell me all this before?"

Birds chirped louder. Gabe stared up at the trees for a moment, then rubbed his forehead, leaving a dirt smudge. "I don't believe in ghosts. And people can't disappear . . ."

Hadley tucked the eye into her pocket. *Yes they can,* she thought.

"Hey," said Gabe. "Wanna help me build a berm to stop the erosion of soil?" He pointed to the edge of her yard. "If not, your house will disappear. Down into the ravine."

Nineteen

The entire house had been painted puce—the color of squashed bedbugs.

Hadley's mother was putting the finishing touches on the walls in the foyer. She looked at Hadley and grinned. "Do you like it? Because if you don't, I'll paint it another color."

"It's fine," said Hadley, though it made her feel like she was standing in an insect slaughterhouse. She couldn't imagine what she had ever liked about the hideous shade.

"I'll get cleaned up and make you some lunch," said her mother, dropping the roller in the tray, splashing droplets of puce on the dark hardwood. "What would you like? Your *wish* is my command."

Hadley flinched. Her eyes arced from floor to ceiling, as though something might magically happen, like the walls shifting or the ceiling caving in. "It doesn't matter," she mumbled. "Just pick something."

"But, darling . . . I wouldn't want you to be disappointed."

Hadley rolled her eyes and sighed out loud. "Fine. Jam and bread."

"Wonderful," said her mother. "Strawberry? Raspberry? Peach?"

"I don't care!" Hadley yelled.

"Don't shout, dear," said her mother, patting Hadley's forehead. "Stress causes wrinkles. I'll get the bread and you get the jam. There are plenty of preserves in the root cellar."

Hadley had never been in the root cellar. Isaac had tried to get her down there several times, but she had refused. She had no desire to go there now, but if she didn't, they'd be arguing all day. About jam.

"When you get back," said her mother, "we'll do each other's nails, and . . ."

Hadley sighed and headed outside.

At the back of the house were two nearly horizontal wooden doors leading down to the cellar. Hadley tugged hard, and they swung open with rickety squeals, revealing concrete steps descending into darkness.

The cramped space was lined with wooden shelves that stretched from floor to ceiling. Each shelf was packed with jars of all shapes and sizes. On the ground were baskets and bushels filled with fruit and vegetables—potatoes, onions, carrots, turnips, and the famous apples Granny used for her crumble.

Hadley reached for a jar labeled *Strawberry.* At the same time the doors above her slammed shut. The jar she was holding smashed at her feet.

She clambered to the top of the steps and pushed as hard as she could, but the doors were stuck. "Help!" she screamed. "Somebody—help! Mom! Gabe!"

Then, one by one, the doors creaked open, and a dark silhouette stood against the bright blue sky.

"What on earth are you doing down there?" said Granny de Mone.

Relief steadied Hadley's trembling hands. "I was getting some jam, and—"

"Jam?" she said. "Heaven knows there's plenty down there. Did you find what you need?"

"Well, yes, but, the doors slammed, and the jar broke, and..."

"That's happened to me a few times. A good strong wind can knock them over. Nearly gave me a heart attack once." She held out a hand and pulled Hadley out of the clammy darkness into the bright sunlight.

Good thing Granny wore her glasses, thought Hadley. The sun was particularly blinding. "Granny—I need to talk to you," she whispered.

Althea de Mone nodded. "Of course. Let's go have a chat."

Together they walked from the cellar to the garage. They climbed the metal steps and entered her apartment. Hadley lowered herself into the sofa cushions, feeling suddenly exhausted, as though she could sink into the floral foam and disappear forever.

"Are you all right? You don't look well. Can I get you a cup of tea?"

Hadley shook her head. "Something's wrong. Things have, well . . . changed."

"Changed?" asked Althea de Mone. "What do you mean *changed*?"

Hadley wanted to tell Granny everything, but she didn't know where to begin. "Nothing's right. Nothing's the same."

Althea de Mone frowned. She patted Hadley's shoulder. "Now, now. Just because something's not the same doesn't make it not right. Sometimes, change can be a good thing. Think of caterpillars."

Hadley wrinkled her brow.

"Caterpillars change, don't they? They become beautiful butterflies."

Hadley pictured a blue butterfly—a *Morpho peleides*—resting on a lower shrub in the understory of a tropical forest in Colombia. Somehow, it made her feel better. It also made her think she'd been spending far too much time with Gabe.

She wanted to ask Granny about Ed and Isaac—she'd made their dolls. She might remember them. She sat up straighter and eyed Granny steadily, looking for any sign of recognition. "Do you, er, know who I live with?"

"Is this a trick question? Or a riddle?" Althea de Mone smiled. "Because I love riddles . . . Now let me think . . ."

"It's not a riddle. Please, Granny. Just answer the question."

"All right, dear. No need to get upset. You live with your mother. Is that the answer you're looking for?"

Hadley sank back into the cushions. There was no point in pressing Granny. The old woman's response would be the same as Gabe's. She took a deep breath and let it out slowly. "Thanks for rescuing me from the cellar."

"Anytime," said Althea de Mone. "And try not to worry so much. I'm sure whatever is bothering you isn't as bad as you believe."

Hadley stood, gave the old woman a hug, and left the apartment.

Her mother was waiting at the front door, still wearing her hair bracelet and tooth necklace. "Did you find some jam?"

"I changed my mind," said Hadley.

"Of course," her mother said. "You're entitled to change your mind. Now, what would you like to eat? I'll make you whatever you want."

Hadley sighed. She said she'd just eat the rest of the peach breakfast—no whipped cream this time.

After they ate, her mother insisted on doing Hadley's nails. She brought a set of clippers, a file, a few shades of polish, and a large, ornate wooden box to the table. She trimmed each of Hadley's nails perfectly. Then Hadley watched in horror as her mother gently scooped up all the clippings, lifted the lid of the ornate box, and placed them inside.

Hadley stood. "I'm going to my room. Don't follow me!"

"Of course," said her mother. "You need your rest. Call if you need anything."

Hadley backed away slowly. She spun on her heels and headed up the stairs.

The walls of the dollhouse were now the color of squashed bedbugs as well. Hadley's mother had painted them puce to match the rest of the house. She bent down and sat beside the small structure.

"This isn't what I wanted," she said out loud. "What I wanted was the perfect family. What I wanted was . . ."

Hadley froze. Why hadn't she thought of it earlier?

Slowly, carefully, she reached a trembling hand into her pocket and pulled out the eye. "This is crazy," she whispered, staring at the eye that stared right back at her.

One simple wish . . . one wish . . . and everything would be perfect.

Twenty

Papa comes home early *from the glasshouse. His head is wrapped in cloth, and two of his workers carry him inside. Doctor Fenton arrives on their heels. There is a terrible, frightening commotion as Frau Heinzelmann and I rush to help.*

The men order me quickly out of the way, and though I retreat a few steps, I linger close enough to watch and listen. They place Papa on the sofa where the doctor attends to his wounds.

There has been a terrible accident at the glasshouse. One of Papa's dog-boys tripped while holding a hot piece of glass. It flew into Papa's face and he was badly injured.

Frau Heinzelmann rouses Mama, and for the first time in over a week she is dressed and out of bed. She and I weep uncontrollably as Doctor Fenton removes the cloth, then cleans and bandages Papa's face. He tells Mama that Papa may lose his right eye, but it is too early to say for certain. Papa will be home for several weeks—perhaps months—while he heals.

Frau Heinzelmann is in a tizzy. She bustles about getting fresh bed linens ready, scrubbing down the bedroom, boiling water for cabbage soup.

That same evening, with Papa tucked into bed, resting, a letter carrier arrives with a telegram for Mama.

She opens it carefully. Before she has finished reading, the paper flutters to the floor. More tears flow down her already red and salt-stained cheeks. She turns to me and says softly, "Pack a bag, little bird. We must head back to Boston. Aunt Cordelia has died of pneumonia."

Twenty-one

The house was suddenly so bright it glowed. Hadley slipped the eye back into her pocket and drew the drapes. Soon she'd need to wear dark glasses—like Granny de Mone.

She stepped into the hall and paused in front of Isaac's room. She held her breath as she pushed open the door. The room was still bare.

As she descended the steps, she became aware of the now-familiar tingling feeling that had traveled from her arm up to her shoulder and down her leg. What was wrong with her? Was she suffering from some kind of strange illness that caused both numbness and hallucinations? It was the most frightening and yet the most plausible explanation.

Hadley's mother stood facing the stove. She had changed clothes. She now wore a floral sundress Hadley had never seen before. And an apron. She rarely wore dresses and she never wore aprons. She looked like she'd walked straight out of an old black-and-white movie—the kind where everyone always looks perfect, even when the world around them is crumbling.

She retrieved a casserole dish from the oven and placed it on the stovetop. At first Hadley worried it was more caramel-peach French toast, but the room didn't smell the least bit sweet.

The table was draped with a starched white tablecloth. Three white plates sat in a perfect triangle. Three sets of cutlery had been placed on white napkins folded precisely and crisply on a diagonal.

Hadley's mother turned slowly. As she drew close, Hadley got a clear look at her face. A polished layer of makeup gave her skin a flawless appearance. Her eyebrows were plucked into thin lines that arched high above her eyes. Pale pink shadow colored her lids and black mascara coated her lashes, making them seem extra thick. Extra long. Her lips were lined and painted to perfection with a muted red lipstick. She looked beautiful. And yet . . . fake.

Hadley cleared her throat. "What's the occasion?"

Her mother smiled. "Just the usual." Her face was porcelain perfect. Hadley was afraid if she smiled too wide it might crack.

Hadley glanced around the kitchen anxiously, and then

lowered herself into a seat. She picked up a knife. She could see her own reflection in the clean, cold steel.

"It's not dinnertime," said her mother, steadying Hadley's hand, gently forcing the knife back into place. "We eat at six p.m. sharp. Not a second earlier."

Hadley cast her a curious look. "What is that?" she said, motioning her chin toward the dish on the stove.

"You know. Quinoa with toasted pine nuts, barley, and vegetables. Your father's favorite side dish."

Hadley barely managed enough spit to swallow. "You mean . . . *Ed?*"

Her mother's eyebrows frowned—though her forehead remained eerily frozen. *"Ed?"*

Hadley's eyes flitted from her mother to the three plates and back again. Her lips parted and moved, but she couldn't manage to form words. She tried harder, but all that came out was an unintelligible squeak.

Her wish. It had come true.

She scanned the kitchen more carefully. The walls were no longer puce. They were pure white. She wasn't sure why she hadn't noticed right away. Something else about the kitchen had changed, too.

The entire room was spotless. Nothing—not one single thing—was out of place. The jars containing sugar and tea and oatmeal were neatly lined on the countertop from largest to smallest. There were no crumbs under the toaster oven, and the cord of the kettle was curled neatly around the handle. The empty steel sink gleamed. The countertop shone. The floor sparkled.

Her mother picked up the knife with the napkin and polished away Hadley's fingerprints, as though getting them out was the only thing that mattered in the world.

"What are you doing?" said Hadley.

"Your father." She smiled. "He's very . . . particular."

Hadley took a deep breath. Her voice was low and wispy. *"Father* . . . Where is he?"

"At work, silly. He'll be home right before dinner. Like clockwork."

Butterflies danced in Hadley's stomach. Her father. Her real father. The man she'd spent her whole life longing to meet—the ghost haunting the hollows of her mind—was somewhere nearby. She was suddenly nervous and excited and a little afraid. She needed to prepare herself. She needed to be ready. She bounced into the hall toward the steps.

"I nearly forgot," called her mother. "Althea de Mone dropped by earlier. She left you a gift. It's near the front door." Then she added quickly, "Make sure you get it before your father trips."

Hadley stopped running. She moved slowly, curiosity drawing her toward the gift as though she were a fish on a wire. As she approached the doll, she drank in every detail—the crisp black suit, the dark hair parted and combed perfectly, and the eyes—the dark eyes—that seemed to be staring right at her.

Hadley had once read that a person's eyes were windows to their soul. Gently, she lifted the doll and held it up to her face. She gazed into its eyes, but they seemed somehow vacant. And cold.

Her emotions flip-flopped. One second, she couldn't wait to meet her real father. The next, she found herself missing Ed and Isaac. So much had changed in so little time; her thoughts and feelings couldn't keep up.

Judging by the doll's size, her father was shorter than Ed, but he was more solid. Ed's doll had been flexible. Her father's doll was rigid. Hadley was afraid if she bent him he would break.

Her mother's words—*not very nice*—hovered in her mind. Hadley smoothed the doll's hair. At least now she could put a face to those words. And there was nothing *not nice* about it. In fact, his face was perfect.

Hadley had always thought she might look a little like her father. A certain slant of the eye. The shape of her lips. Perhaps her long, skinny feet. But there was no resemblance. She couldn't help but feel a twinge of disappointment.

She walked up the stairs and into her room. Gently, she

placed her father's doll in the dollhouse living room. She moved her mother to sit across from him.

Hadley took a deep breath. Her mother said he'd come home just before dinner. She had most of the afternoon to sit around and wait. She had to find something to occupy her time or she'd drive herself crazy—assuming she wasn't already there.

Granny, she thought. *I'll ask her about the doll.*

Hadley's mother had left the kitchen. She was now vacuuming the living room. Buckets, dusters, and an array of cleaning products lined the hallway. It was like she had turned into some kind of cleaning machine. Hadley was afraid to touch anything.

She left the house quietly and walked around the side. In the room above the garage, the dark drapes hung heavy and straight without even the slightest hint of movement behind them. Hadley climbed the metal steps leading to Granny's apartment. Just as she reached the top, the screen door swung open. It knocked against the metal railing, tap, tap, tapping in the breeze. The wooden door was also ajar.

Hadley stuck her head inside. "Hello?" she called, but no one answered.

Perhaps Granny was in the bathroom or cleaning her closet. Hadley shifted her weight, suddenly worried. Had something gone wrong with her wish? Had Granny disappeared, too?

Invading someone's private space was wrong. Hadley recalled how angry she'd always been with Isaac each time he'd barged uninvited into her room. But she convinced herself this was different. She had to make sure Granny was all right. That Granny was still there.

Hadley took a few tentative steps into the apartment, carefully searching the space. The bed was perfectly made, the sheets forming tight corners, the pillows fluffed to perfection. No knickknacks or magazines cluttered the sofa or coffee table. The kitchen was spotless, as though it had never been used.

Thunk.

Hadley searched the room for the cause of the sound. Nothing had fallen. Nothing was out of place. She searched again, her eyes coming to rest on the old steamer trunk. It was larger than she'd remembered—big enough to fit a whole person in it.

It was made of dark rustic wood, weathered and worn. The sides were bound and riveted with tarnished metal, and the hinges were uneven—as though a blacksmith had forged them a hundred years ago. It reminded Hadley of a pirate's chest.

She reached out a trembling hand and pulled the clasp. Before she could lift the heavy lid, a hand touched her shoulder. She spun around, nearly falling backward over the trunk. Granny held her arm and steadied her.

"Hadley," she said. "How nice of you to pop by again."

"I—um—I'm sorry, I..." Hadley struggled to explain why she was inside Granny's apartment without permission.

"Nothing to be sorry about," said Granny de Mone.

"I didn't mean to barge in. I couldn't find you and I was worried."

"You're such a dear," she said. "I was cleaning the root cellar. A glass of jam had smashed. It was all over the floor." She placed an armful of apples on the counter. They were red and shiny and perfect.

"Well, the door was open, and I didn't see you, and I heard a sound." Hadley pointed to the old trunk. "What's in there?"

"Just my carving tools and sewing kit—to make the dolls. And speaking of dolls, did you get my gift?"

"Yes," said Hadley. "That's why I came..."

"I knew you'd like it. You can add it to the others. Your mother. And me. I'm sorry I haven't finished your doll yet. Just a few more touches and it should be ready."

Hadley smiled vaguely.

"Then we'll be the perfect family, won't we?" She gave Hadley a squeeze. "Have a seat, dear, and I'll make you some tea."

She walked to the kitchenette, pulled a kettle from a cupboard, and filled it with water. She put some herbs into the silver teapot and added the water once it boiled. The scent was soothing. Granny served the tea and Hadley took a sip.

"Granny?" she asked. "Tell me more about the house. About the previous owners. Did they ever, well, say anything *strange* had happened? Why did so many of them abandon the place?"

Granny dropped her chin. "You've been listening to gossip."

Hadley sat back on the sofa. "Maybe. But are you sure nothing strange ever happened to anyone else?"

"Well . . . ," she said slowly. "Remember I told you the original owner had the house built for his wife—to make her happy? And the dollhouse was a gift to his daughter? His only child?"

Hadley nodded, hanging on her every word.

"Well, the daughter—supposedly a lovely girl—well, one day, she was gone."

Hadley swallowed. Her voice trembled. "Gone? As in *disappeared*?"

Granny shook her head slowly. "Gone as in died. Her parents went mad with grief. The woman had to be sent to a sanatorium. The father deserted the house, leaving everything behind. The furniture. Even the food in the pantry and cellar."

Hadley shivered. Someone was dancing on her grave.

"They say the house sat empty for a long time after that. Like an old abandoned seashell. Then, new people bought it. They weren't happy here either and left quickly. There have been several owners since."

Hadley sat deep in thought. "What an awful story."

Granny patted her knee. "That was a long time ago. Don't think about it. You're here now and everything is fine. Think happy thoughts."

Hadley wondered what had happened to the girl. She put her hand in her pocket and withdrew the eye.

"Where did you find that?" asked Granny.

Hadley held it up for Granny to see. "Under my bed. Does it belong to you? Did it come from one of your dolls?"

"Perhaps," said Granny, closing Hadley's fingers around the eye. "But you keep it for now. I'll try and locate a matching one, and then I'll show you how I make the dolls. Would you like that?"

Hadley forced a smile.

Granny de Mone placed a hand to her mouth and yawned. "Another time. We'll make dolls and play pinochle, and I'll bake another crumble."

Twenty-two

Are you just going to stand there, or are you going to help?" said Gabe, holding out an extra shovel.

Hadley had gone inside the house to find her mother was busy dusting, cleaning, and disinfecting as though her very life depended on it. She'd made Hadley a peanut butter sandwich for a snack, cutting it into perfect triangles, and asked her to eat it outside so she wouldn't make any mess. Hadley had taken it into the backyard, where she sat on the rock enjoying the breeze.

"Can I finish my sandwich first?" she huffed. "It's attracting flies."

"Is there any meat in it?" Gabe asked, tossing the shovel near her feet.

"It's peanut butter."

Gabe shook his head. "I told you before—these are flesh

flies. Blowflies. They're attracted to rotting flesh. That, and dung."

"Stop talking about dung while I'm eating," said Hadley, shoving the rest of her sandwich into her mouth. She couldn't help but think of Isaac and his peanut allergy. She missed Isaac—his annoying questions, his allergies...and his freckles.

Hadley kicked off her sneakers and dangled her feet over the rock. Her one leg still felt odd. She really should see a doctor.

She swallowed her last bite and jumped into the long grass. It was cool and damp against the soles of her feet. Dirt squished between her toes. It was icky and nice at the same time.

"What are we doing again?" she asked, stepping into her sneakers and picking up the shovel.

"We're building a berm."

"Right. And what exactly is a berm?"

"The earth is eroding. Right here." Gabe pointed to the edge of the yard. "Fast-flowing rainwater's carved away the soil. A hundred years ago, your yard was a lot longer. It stretched out over where we're standing. A good chunk of it has dropped off into the ravine."

"Really?" said Hadley, peering down.

"That's nothing. In a thousand years, your whole yard

will be gone. Your house will drop off into the ravine, too. Unless . . ."

Hadley sighed. "We build a berm."

Gabe nodded. "First, we start at the base with a retaining wall. We'll build the berm later, to redirect the flow of water from the top of your yard."

Together they scoured the ravine, digging up as many rocks as they could find and dragging them back to the slope. Hadley kept an eye out for thistles and poison ivy, not to mention snakes and giant centipedes.

They worked side by side, placing the rocks on the slope, building up a small wall. They also dug up soil and moved it to the side of the ravine. They pulled up chunks of wild grass by the roots and relocated it to the slope as well. Gabe said the roots of certain plants would help bind the soil so it wouldn't erode.

Hadley didn't bother telling Gabe about her father. He didn't remember Ed or Isaac so she figured there was no use. She did tell him about the original owners of the house and their daughter who died.

"Wow," he said. "If I believed in ghosts, I'd say your house *was* haunted." He yanked out a clump of weeds and tucked it into some soil between the rocks. "But I don't believe in ghosts."

They worked for a long time, but the wall of rock was

still small. Hadley wiped the sweat from her forehead. The berm was going to take forever.

She swatted at a fly buzzing near her ear just as she jabbed her shovel into the hard soil. It struck a hard patch of clay and stuck. She grabbed the handle and pulled, but the shovel wouldn't budge. She pulled harder, her hands slippery from sandwich and sweat, and lost her grip. She flew backward into Gabe. They toppled to the ground.

"Hey!" he said, shoving her aside. "Watch what you're doing."

Hadley got to her feet. She was covered in dirt. She tried smacking it off her T-shirt and shorts, but that only made it worse.

Gabe stood and walked toward the shovel. He pulled it free and began examining the earth where it had gotten stuck.

"I gotta go," said Hadley. It was getting late. It was almost dinnertime. She didn't want to meet her real father for the first time looking like something the cat dragged in. She'd best head inside, get cleaned up, and change.

"But," said Gabe, "what about the berm?"

"I'll help you tomorrow," she called over her shoulder. She scaled the embankment and headed for the side door.

Hadley kicked off her shoes in the front foyer after having trekked through the hall, leaving a trail of muddy prints.

Before she reached the stairs, her mother stepped out

from the living room. She looked at the floor; panic flashed in her eyes.

Realizing what she'd done, Hadley was about to tell her not to worry, that she'd clean the dirt right away. But before she could manage a word, another figure appeared behind her mother. He wore a crisp black suit. He had perfect hair and a perfect face.

Twenty-three

Hello, Doll Face."

Hadley gawked at the man who had only lived in the misty corners of her imagination. He looked identical to the doll, as if it had ballooned in size and sprung to life. All other thoughts were wiped clean from her mind.

He smiled warmly. Then his gaze slipped from her face to her dirty clothes. It lingered for a moment near her feet, and then followed the path of muddy footprints she'd left along the hall floor. Hadley was sure a twitch tugged once at the corner of his mouth.

"Why, you're filthy," he said quietly. "And what in the world are you wearing?"

Hadley looked down at her T-shirt and shorts. She folded her arms nervously around herself.

"Oh, never mind," he said, sidestepping Hadley's mother. "Come here."

He put an arm around her shoulder. He had strong arms, and Hadley found herself comparing them to Ed's loosey-goosey arms that could coil around her a thousand times and still provide no pressure.

"I feel like I haven't seen you in a thousand years," he whispered.

Though he was a complete stranger, it somehow didn't feel that way. This was her father. Her *real* father. He was here and he was hugging her and suddenly nothing else mattered. She breathed in his clean scent. He smelled like a freshly unwrapped bar of spring-scented soap.

"Try twelve," she muttered.

He stepped back, dusting a speck of dirt from his suit. "Twelve what?"

She grinned. "Er, nothing."

Hadley wanted him to go on hugging her forever, but she tried not to look too eager. Still, she couldn't take her eyes off him—his clean-shaved, sculpted jaw, his friendly eyes, and the smile that wrapped itself around her like a warm woolly blanket. He was everything she'd hoped he'd be. He was perfect.

"I'm so efficient. I got everything done a whole half hour ahead of schedule today, so I thought I'd come home early to be with my girls," he said, flashing a smile at Hadley's mother. "I thought we might go for a walk or have a game of cards or sit around and chat before dinner."

He tilted his head toward the dirt Hadley had dragged into the house. He raised one eyebrow. "But you've got some cleaning to do first, missy."

"I'll get that," said her mother, but before she could move an inch, he reached out and barred her path.

"Hadley can do it," he said sweetly. "She's old enough to clean her own messes."

"Of course, dear," said her mother. "You're right, as usual."

"Sure," said Hadley, grinning. She didn't want to take her eyes off him in case he up and disappeared like Ed and Isaac. "I can do it."

Hadley walked toward her parents and they parted to let her pass. Still keeping one eye on her father, she bent and grabbed a rag and a bucket her mother had left near the array of cleaning products.

The disinfectant stung her hand as she dunked the rag into the bucket and wrung it dry. Her father stood over her, watching as she backtracked, wiping every single one of the dirty footprints. It was strange how he watched without helping, but she guessed he was just one of those supervising types.

When she finished, she stood and gave him a satisfied smile, but he stared back at her, unblinking. Hadley searched the now glistening wet floor and then his face for a clue as to what he might want her to do next. He waited patiently, as though she were supposed to figure this out for herself. All the while, Hadley's mother continued to smile, but her eyes snuck to Hadley's feet and then back to her eyes as if to tell her something.

Then it hit her—her feet! The soles were brown with ground-in dirt.

"What are you going to do now, genius?" said her father.

"Oops." She laughed nervously. "Do you think you could toss me some paper towels?"

Her mother made a move, but her father stopped her again.

"Hadley has gotten herself into this mess—literally." He chuckled. "It's up to her to get herself out."

He turned and disappeared up the stairs, whistling cheerfully. Hadley's mother picked up an armful of spray bottles, winked, and escaped into the kitchen.

How strange, thought Hadley. Then she gave her head a shake and plunked one foot straight into the bucket, washing off the dirt. She rinsed the other foot and then wiped the puddle of water beneath her feet. She threw the rag into the bucket and took it to the bathroom in the hall, where she flushed the dirt and water down the toilet. She wrung out the rag and folded it neatly, draping it along the rim of the bucket.

She stole a glance at herself in the mirror. Her hair was a

mess. She smoothed it with her palm, straightened her T-shirt, and checked her shorts for stains. She didn't want to disappoint her father. She could hear him whistling cheerfully in his room.

She headed toward the kitchen and peered through the doorway, where her mother sat at the perfectly set table, staring straight ahead, her hands folded in front of her, smiling at the wall.

Hadley shook her head. She walked to the stairs and tiptoed upward. She would clean herself up and put on something nice. She was excited to spend more time with her father—find out more about who he really was. As she stepped into her room, the smile slipped from her lips.

Lying neatly across her duvet, as though someone had set it out for her to wear, was a frilly pink dress. It was a tea-length cupcake style—like nothing Hadley had ever owned, let alone worn before. The sleeveless bodice was fitted, with a diamond pattern stitched in fine silk thread. A tulle underskirt added extra fullness to the billowing organza pleats. It looked like something a doll would wear.

Twenty-four

Mama and I arrive home from Boston. Papa is still bedridden. His wound has become infected, and Doctor Fenton tells Mama he is making the necessary preparations to remove Papa's eye in the morning. Mama faints upon receiving the frightful news, but Frau Heinzelmann is there to catch her.

Frau Heinzelmann forces me to eat a warm bowl of beef stew filled with carrots and potatoes. I take only a few bites, while Mama cannot eat at all. She is weary from the long journey and retires to her room. The listlessness that had briefly left her has returned.

While Frau Heinzelmann clears the dishes, I sit alone by the fireplace, warming my hands. My dollhouse remains where I left it weeks ago. I reach inside to pull out the doll Papa made for me but I startle. Sitting next to the doll, glaring at me with its black eyes, is the creature with pale limbs and ghostly white hair.

"I have come to claim my ransom," it says in a small voice.

I nearly fall backward, but I steady myself and gather my courage. "But you did not fulfill your end of the bargain, and therefore I owe you nothing."

"Ah, but I did," it hisses. "You asked that your father be home. And so he is. You wanted your mother out of her bed. So she was. And did you not return to your beloved Boston?"

I think of all that has happened and it suddenly occurs to me that my wishes—they did come true after all, only not in the manner I had intended.

"But . . . but . . ." My voice trembles. "That was not what I meant . . ."

"The how is not important," says the creature, "simply the what. You have received all you asked for. Now you must give me something in return." It grins wickedly.

I turn my back on the dollhouse. My mind scrambles for a way out of my bargain. I did indeed ask for Papa to be home, and for Mama to be up, and to return to Boston. But I also asked for one more thing.

"You did not deliver all I asked," I say. "You did not provide me with a friend."

When I turn toward the dollhouse, my doll is alone. The creature has vanished.

I almost feel I have escaped it when all at once I feel a cold breath on my shoulder. I spin around to discover, standing full-size by the fireplace, a girl. She wears a pretty dress, and her silky white hair pours loosely down her back. Only her cavernous eyes give her away.

"I shall be your friend," she says in a sweet voice. "For now. And for always." She reaches out to touch my arm. Her touch prickles my skin and chills me to the bone. "But come now, first you must pay me what you owe."

"And w-what is that?" I ask, taking a step backward.

"Why, your eyes, of course," she says, smiling. "I would like a beautiful pair of silver-gray eyes to call my own."

The creature reaches her dainty hands toward my face, but I draw back farther, nearly stumbling over the dollhouse. All the while my mind works feverishly to win time. She reaches a second time, her sharp claws grazing my cheek, which immediately turns icy. With my back already against the wall, there is nowhere for me to go.

"Give me one day," I say quickly. "Removing one's eyes is not an easy feat. Allow me to prepare for the removal, and I swear I will pay what I owe."

The girl pauses as if to ponder my request. Then, backing away slightly, she tilts her head and agrees. "I give you *twenty-four hours to honor your bargain. Twenty-four hours. No more."*

Relief washes over me. I have won a reprieve. But I know my relief will be short-lived when she adds, "Just remember, if you do not fulfill your promise and deliver your eyes to me of your own free will—then I shall claim them myself." She fans her dainty hand with tiny claw-like nails and grins.

Twenty-five

Hadley trod ever so lightly down the steps, like Cinderella making her grand entrance into the ball.

The organza dress rustled. It was tight and horribly uncomfortable. The neckline itched, but Hadley didn't dare scratch, because once she started, she'd never be able to stop. She kept asking herself why she'd put on the darn thing, but the answer was simple—she wore it to please her father, because she was somehow sure it was what he wanted.

Reaching the threshold to the living room, Hadley paused. She took a deep breath and smoothed her hair. Her father sat on the sofa reading a newspaper. As she stepped inside, he looked up at her and his eyes lit up like summer sparklers.

"You look beautiful, Doll Face," he said. "Perfectly radiant." He motioned for her to sit beside him.

Hadley's cheeks flushed. She'd met with his approval.

Slowly, carefully, as though treading on eggshells, she moved toward him and settled into the comfy sofa by his side.

He set down the newspaper and put an arm around her. "I can't believe how grown-up you're getting. It seems like only yesterday you were a baby ... spitting up all over me, drooling, and all that other disgusting stuff."

Hadley blinked, trying hard not to let a frown muscle its way through her bright smile. What was so horrible about babies? Throwing up and drooling was what they did. She inched ever so slightly away, but he drew her back in tight.

"How about a game of cards before dinner?" he asked. "Or that kite I gave you last week—how about we try to fly it?"

Hadley's body went rigid. A kite. He wanted to fly a kite. Just like Ed and Isaac. She sighed softly. Ed and Isaac ...

Hadley wanted to tell her father she'd rather do something else, but there was a look in his eye she couldn't quite identify. A look that told her she'd best not disappoint him.

He hauled her to her feet, only they didn't seem to want to cooperate. She nearly tipped sideways, but luckily he caught hold of her.

"You're like a bull in ballet slippers," he chuckled.

Hadley's mother poked her head into the room. "Where are you two off to?"

Her voice was an echo of what it used to be. There was no strength in it. No assuredness.

"Shouldn't you be making dinner?" Her father winked. "I'm getting hungry."

"Of course, dear." She smiled. "I'm making all your favorites."

Hadley's lips were sewn tight. This mother was unrecognizable. Her face was not her own. Her voice was someone else's. The mother she knew would never have responded that way. The mother she knew would have said something like, *If you're so hungry, why don't you get up off that sofa and help so we can get it done quicker?*

Now that she had her real father, Hadley found herself missing her real mother—the strong, fearless parking enforcer who would give tickets to truck drivers and UPS deliverers and order them to move their vehicles. This new mother couldn't command a fly. Hadley gazed at the impostor with a mixture of disappointment and contempt.

Hadley's father pulled her by the upper arm and together they headed toward the door. She slipped into a pair of shiny black patent-leather shoes that sat waiting. She'd never owned a pair of patent-leather shoes in her life, but these seemed to fit perfectly.

She followed her father around the side of the house. He went straight to the garage and yanked open the door. The old mess had been replaced with absolute order. Hadley gawked at the floor—it was so clean you could eat off it.

At the far end three bins formed a perfect line. Two blue

recycling boxes—one labeled *Paper* and another labeled *Plastic*—sat side by side. A green bin labeled *Compost* completed the trio. Any rusty old gardening tools that had littered the floor were now good as new and hung neatly on a system of hooks along the walls. Even the old croquet and badminton sets Hadley had played with were now sitting neatly on a wooden shelf.

Her father walked to the back and located a kite. It was the same blue-and-orange one Ed and Isaac had been trying to fly that afternoon that now felt like centuries ago. Pangs of guilt jabbed at her insides.

"There's no wind," she said quietly, as they stepped into the yard, but even before she finished her sentence, a gentle breeze blew softly across her face.

"There's enough," said her father, chuckling. He walked to the center of the lawn. "Perfect weather to fly a kite."

"Perfect," echoed Hadley.

He handed Hadley the spindle and walked to the back of the yard, as the string unspooled in her hands. And then, like some bizarre déjà vu, he motioned for her to run with the spindle to force the kite airborne. Hadley turned, trying not to let him see her face. She missed Ed. He never ordered her mother around. He made her mother smile.

"All right," said her father. "Go!"

Hadley had no choice but to run, her pink organza dress billowing around her. The neckline grated against her skin, but she resisted the urge to scratch. The string behind her pulled tight and the kite sailed upward. Her father shouted encouraging things like, "Great job, Hadley! Keep going!"

Then, like Ed, she turned at the wrong moment, and she tripped over her own feet. She fell hard, sliding along the ground.

The words of praise stopped immediately.

Hadley lay there, catching her breath, staring at the cloudless blue sky. She remembered how Ed and Isaac and her mother had laughed. It made her smile. She closed her eyes. The sunshine was warm and bright on her face, until a shadow crept over her.

Her father loomed, his face pinched and red. He grabbed her shoulders and hoisted her to her feet.

"You're as clumsy as a cow," he said. "Don't you know how to do something as simple as fly a kite?"

Hadley shrank from his hot breath that jabbed at her with each word.

"I—I just," she stammered. "My feet—they got tangled..."

"Look at you," he said, roughly brushing dirt from her dress. "Look what you've done."

Hadley noticed there was a tiny rip in the seam near her shoulder. She raised her hand to inspect the damage, but her father pushed it aside.

"You've ruined it," he said.

"It—it's okay, Dad," said Hadley. "I can fix it. Honestly.

I can sew it and it will look good as new." Her lips quivered, but she commanded them to smile just one second longer.

"Fine," he said, stepping away. "You do that. And clean this mess." He pointed to the tangled kite string and the blue-orange battered lump lying in the grass. "Throw it out and take the bins to the curb. Tomorrow is garbage day. We wouldn't want to miss getting rid of all that trash."

"Sure," she said, her voice trembling slightly. Hadley forced her smile to freeze in place. One more second. Just one more. And then he turned his back, and her jaw muscles went limp.

Hadley gripped the spindle and began winding the string, moving at a steady pace toward the kite. She breathed deeply, trying to decipher what had gone so terribly wrong. She hoped Gabe wouldn't show up. The last thing she needed was for him to see her wearing this ridiculous dress.

Inside the garage, she tossed the broken kite into one of the recycling bins. She began lugging the one labeled *Plastic* toward the curb. She returned for the green compost bin, and then the one labeled *Paper*. She plunked it down at the curb beside the other two. Satisfied, she wiped her hands on her dress.

She was about to turn when the top newspaper in the recycling bin caught her attention. The heading read: *MISS-ING*. It was the newspaper from some time ago—the one Al-thea de Mone had handed her mother the first day they'd met.

Hadley lifted the paper and stared at the photo under-neath the headline. It was of a man, a woman, and a little girl. The paper slipped from her hands and fluttered to the ground. They were identical to the family of dolls that had disappeared from her dollhouse.

Twenty-six

Hadley picked up the needle and thread her mother had given her. She slipped out of the dress and put on a clean pair of shorts and a fresh T-shirt. It was like she was stepping out of someone else's skin and back into her own.

Carefully, she mended the rip in the dress as best she could. When she was finished, there was a jagged line of uneven stitches. She turned the dress over in her hands and noticed a small grass stain on the back of it. Good thing her father hadn't seen that or who knows what he might have done.

Carrying the dress into the bathroom, she wet a corner of a towel and then rubbed it with soap. She dabbed the stain, careful not to harm the delicate fabric. When she was sure the dress looked as good as it was ever going to she took it back to her room and laid it on her bed, dreading the thought of putting it back on.

Hadley sat beside the dollhouse. The three dolls were exactly where she'd left them. What had happened to the family that had lived in the house before her? What had happened to their dolls? For the first time she believed Isaac. He hadn't taken them.

Her father bellowed up the long dark staircase, announcing it was time for dinner. The sharpness in his voice told Hadley he didn't intend to call a second time.

The dress felt tighter and more uncomfortable than ever. The neckline was now like sandpaper. She quickly combed her hair, her scalp stinging with each knot she yanked out.

Hadley's knees trembled as she made her way into the kitchen. The air was thick with the aroma of roasted meat. Her mother stood at the counter, placing the quinoa mixture into a bowl. Her father sat at the table, waiting.

Hadley eyed the crisp white cloth, the starched linen napkins, and the gleaming cutlery. She recalled how Ed and Isaac and her mother had sat there not long ago, laughing, eating, playing board games. Though she had been starving, her appetite was suddenly gone.

"You're late," said her father.

"Late?" she asked.

"Don't talk back to me."

Hadley scurried to the chair beside him.

"You've fixed your dress," he said, flicking a finger at the jagged seam. He was smiling, but it wasn't a warm smile like the first time she'd seen him. It was more of a sneer.

"Well?" he said. He looked toward Hadley's mother expectantly.

She practically jumped, spun around, and brought over the bowl of quinoa. She set it down, smiled, and then was off again to grab a platter of thinly sliced rare roast beef. A bowl of salad sat waiting on the table, and when Hadley reached for it, her father's head snapped in her direction. She withdrew her hand as though it had been smacked.

As soon as Hadley's mother slipped into her seat beside her father, he reached for the salad bowl and placed a large helping on his plate first. Next, he served her mother, and last he served Hadley.

Hadley watched her mother carefully, waiting for some kind of cue as to when she might be allowed to begin, but she just sat there staring off into space, smiling.

As soon as Hadley's father picked up his fork, her mother did the same. Hadley took hers quickly, too, as though she had to keep up. A sprinkling of sweat dampened her forehead. She had never worked so hard at eating a meal before.

Biting daintily into a wedge of cucumber, Hadley snuck a sideways glance at her father. A fly zipped about his face. At first he made no move to shoo it, then in one swift motion, he caught the insect in his fist. Hadley watched as he slowly squeezed the life out of it, then placed it into his napkin and handed it to Hadley's mother to dispose of.

Hadley's stomach turned. Suddenly she was desperate to leave. She stood, but her father slammed his fist once onto the table. The china plates and glasses clinked in shock. Hadley stood statue-still, unable to leave and unable to sit. Her father resumed eating like nothing had happened. Hadley met her mother's gaze, and their eyes locked for an instant.

Say something, Hadley willed. *Do something.* But her mother just smiled that same synthetic smile as though everything were simply perfect.

"I—I need to go to the bathroom," Hadley stammered, as soon as she could get her mouth to cooperate.

"Of course," her father said gently. "But don't take too long. You wouldn't want your dinner to get cold."

Hadley forced her feet to move slowly, steadily, until she was safely in the hall, and then she dashed up the stairs and into the bathroom, locking the door behind her.

She turned on the tap and splashed cold water onto her face, not caring if it soaked her dress in the process. She swallowed great gulps of air, and when she'd managed to catch her breath and calm her stomach, she sat on the edge of the tub.

If nothing else, she now had a very clear picture of what *not very nice* meant. *Not very nice* meant a pathological obsession with neatness. *Not very nice* meant prone to bouts of explosive rage. *Not very nice* meant cruel words and behavior. Hadley's real father was *not very nice*. She should have left it at that.

Hadley managed to avoid her parents for the rest of the evening. She told them she was sick to her stomach. It was the truth.

As twilight smeared a hazy film over the neighborhood, she stared at the street. More than ever, she longed for the apartment in the city. For the noisy traffic, the stinky sewers, the bicycles and pedestrians that made it impossible to feel lonely.

She found the eye in the pocket of her shorts and nearly made another wish. She quickly stopped herself. Each time she had made a wish, it hadn't turned out the way she'd expected. Grace was right—she should never have begun wishing.

She gazed out the window, setting her sight on the bins lining the curb. The idea came to her so suddenly it nearly knocked her over.

"It's time to take out the trash," she said, grinning.

Twenty-seven

Hadley lay in bed pretending to sleep. She nearly nodded off several times, but each time she pinched herself hard to keep awake.

Her mother came into the room to check on her. She kissed Hadley gently on the cheek and then pulled the duvet over her shoulders. She exited the room as quietly as she'd entered.

Her father came as well. Steady footsteps approached from the hall. They stopped and the door glided open. He didn't set foot inside; he just stood there. Though Hadley didn't dare open her eyes, she was certain it was him.

She lay perfectly still, commanding every muscle in her body to obey. It seemed like an eternity until the door closed again and the footsteps disappeared down the hall. Her lungs deflated slowly. She'd been holding her breath.

Once she was certain they were asleep, she got up and hoisted the dollhouse and exited her room. Hadley swayed under its weight. It was heavier and more awkward to handle than it had been the first time she'd lifted it.

The hall was empty. She took several steps, and then the floorboards yelped beneath her feet. She froze for seconds that felt like hours, but nothing stirred. She moved again, this time inching across the landing toward the stairs.

Slowly, carefully, she began her descent. Reaching the bottom step, she moved silently to the front door. There, she set the house on the floor and shook her arms. They were both hollow and tingly.

She clicked the deadbolt and pulled as hard as she could, but the door stuck. It didn't want to budge. She tried again and again, but it wouldn't open, so she propped her foot against the wall to brace herself. When she tugged with every last bit of strength in her body, the door flew open, and Hadley stumbled backward, landing next to the dollhouse.

She found herself face-to-face with the doll that looked like her father. He glared at her, like he knew exactly what she was up to.

Hadley found her feet and slowly backed away, half expecting the man to appear at the top of the steps. She took a few breaths and pulled herself together. Picking up the doll-house, she plunged through the open door.

The evening air was warm and moist. Other than the song of a few crickets, the street seemed eerily quiet. She lugged the dollhouse all the way to the curb without stopping. She plunked it beside the neat line of recycling bins.

She tucked the glass eye inside her dollhouse bedroom, under the bed. She dusted off her hands, grinning. Once the eye and the house were destroyed, the spell would be broken, and things would go back to normal.

Halfway up the drive, Hadley remembered the dolls. The memory of Isaac's busted ankle flashed through her brain. She ran back to the curb and snatched her mother's doll and Granny's. She left her father's doll right where he was.

"We wouldn't want to miss getting rid of all that trash," she said out loud. A sliver of delight curled her lips.

Hadley scurried up the driveway and into the house. She shut the door behind her, careful not to let it slam. Back in her bedroom, Hadley gently placed the dolls on her dresser. She slipped beneath her covers and closed her eyes.

Hadley dreamed she was standing at the curb. The garbage truck was stopped in front of the house. It was grinding and chewing and churning the trash. But as it drove off, something crawled out from the back.

Twenty-eight

Hadley **awoke to a grinding sound.** Wheels, cogs, bolts—all churning and writhing and screeching as they spun and turned and tightened. A blast of exhaust ended the metallic symphony. The garbage truck had arrived.

Hadley made it to the window in time to see the truck trundle on its way. The bins lay upside down at the edge of the drive. Though she only had a narrow view, there was no sign of the dollhouse. She breathed a sigh of relief.

It was over. The house was gone. The eye was gone. Her father's doll was gone. Maybe everything would go back to normal now. Maybe getting rid of them would break the spell. Hadley's heart inflated. It floated to the ceiling like a bright pink balloon. Then she turned her head, and with a sharp stab the balloon popped.

The dollhouse sat in the exact spot it had sat for the past week.

"I—I got rid of you," she said, stepping back. "I put you at the curb . . . *Didn't I?*"

Hadley was lost in a mental maze, and she was terrified she'd never find her way out. Had she really left her room last night? Had she really put the dollhouse by the trash? Or had she fallen asleep and dreamed the entire thing? Her stomach churned. She wasn't sure anymore.

She heard a long drawn-out rumble. She turned slowly to see the eye rolling toward her across the floor.

Hadley threw on some clothes and raced out of her room. She flew down the stairs, jumped into her shoes, and tugged at the front door. It was sealed tight, as though the house didn't want her to leave.

She managed to pry it open and dashed out into the open air. She didn't stop running until she was at the edge of the ravine. But even that wasn't far enough.

Stones and twigs jabbed into the soles of her feet as she slid down the embankment and into the gully. She rested only once the house was completely out of sight—hidden by the thick intertwining branches and layers of deep green leaves.

Sitting on the trunk of a fallen tree, she closed her eyes. She breathed in the musky odor of decaying wood and damp earth. The slow trickle of water from the nearby creek soothed her mind. Birds chirped. Leaves rustled. She could sort this all out—maybe even come up with some kind of a plan—if only she could stay away long enough.

"Hadley!"

Her eyes snapped open.

"Haaadleeeey!"

The sound of his voice stopped her heart cold.

Hadley dove for cover, pressing herself flat against the rough bark of the old log. She swallowed great gulps of air, but it was as though there wasn't enough oxygen left in the universe to fill half her lungs. She crouched, prepared to spring into action in case he came after her.

"It's Daddy, Doll Face. I want to talk to you."

His voice was distant, as though it were coming from down a deep, deep well. The heady scent of moss and toadstools filled her nostrils as she squashed herself into the damp earth. Using her elbows, she inched along the ground until she was safely hidden behind the fat, gnarly trunk of an old tree. Slowly, she lifted herself and poked her head around it.

Through the tangle of leaves, she could see a figure at the edge of the ravine. She could barely make out the shape, but there was no mistaking it.

"Hadley, honey! I have something I want to give you."

Hadley ducked back behind the tree. Air moved in and out of her lungs in ragged, wheezing puffs. She couldn't have seen right, she told herself. She snuck another peek.

"Come home, Hadley."

His voice remained sweet, his words calm. If she didn't know any better, she'd have sworn he was looking to give her a hug and maybe some kind of a treat. Her heart drummed a warning in her chest. There was no treat waiting for her there.

Time melted into a dark puddle of dread. Hadley let herself sink into it.

"Okay," he said finally. "But remember, you can't stay down there forever."

Maybe not, she thought. *But I can try.*

"I'll be in the house," he said calmly. "Waiting."

His last word seemed to echo on and on inside her head until it finally disappeared, taking with it all the sounds in the universe. Nothing around her stirred. The birds had stopped chirping. The insects had stopped buzzing. Even the air stopped circulating and felt heavy and stagnant. It was as though time had frozen and Hadley was encased in its ice.

After what seemed like forever, she gathered enough courage to move. Slowly, she poked her head out and risked another look. The upper edge of the ravine was empty. Only the top of the house was visible—the Cyclops eye glaring at her like the sharp beam of a lighthouse.

"Hey."

Hadley's heart leaped into her lungs. She spun around.

As soon as her brain registered who was standing there, she lunged for him, grabbed his T-shirt, and yanked.

"Come on."

Hadley ran as fast as she could, dragging Gabe along with her. He followed without question—as though the look on her face had been enough to tell him something was terribly wrong.

Deeper and deeper into the woods they fled. Gabe took the lead as they wove around old trunks, avoided low-hanging branches, waded through thick weeds, and jumped over tangled roots.

When they finally arrived at a clearing, Hadley slowed to a jog. The creek wasn't far ahead. She reached the bank just in time to collapse on the edge, gasping for air.

Gabe dropped down beside her. He sucked in great gulps. "W-what's g-going on? Are you out of your m-mind?"

"Maybe," she said, her chest rising and falling as she attempted to catch her own breath.

The sun beamed down from a cloudless blue. A soft breeze blew hot and dry against Hadley's skin. But instead of making her feel cheerful, it had the opposite effect. She had become suspicious of anything too bright, too beautiful, too clean—or too perfect.

"Gabe?" she said once she was calm enough to speak.

"Yeah?"

A million thoughts battled to be first out of her mouth, but they got tangled and stuck in her throat. She was desperate to tell Gabe everything. Tell him there was no such thing as reality—that reality was a gossamer fabric that could easily wrinkle or snag and tear. She wanted to tell him that life, as she knew it, had been altered, and that everyone around her—even he, Gabe—had been affected by the change. But where would she start? And would he only think she was crazy?

Hadley took a deep breath and sighed. She wasn't even sure she believed herself anymore. "Forget it," she said, picking up a rock and tossing it into the creek.

Gabe, who had been observing her all the while, narrowed his eyes. Then he picked up a rock as well and tossed it into the creek. It splashed into the water in the exact spot hers had entered.

They sat there, side by side, not saying a word for the longest time. And Hadley thought about all that had happened. And why it had happened.

Why had she been so unhappy? Ed had been good to her. He had been trying hard to get closer. And Isaac was cute. And it was nice to have a little brother to share things with and teach things to and even argue with. And though Gabe was no replacement for Sydney, he was kind of funny, and only a bit weird, and Hadley had decided she liked bugs—at least some kinds. And the house was big, and the yard was beautiful, and the leafy suburb was much quieter than the apartment in the city. Why had she wished her new life away? Why couldn't she just have been happy?

As she sat there pondering how it had all gone so wrong, she threw rocks and twigs into the flowing water. She shredded wild grass until her fingers turned a sickly green, tossing the strands into the water and watching them sail onward, imagining them drifting all the way to the Monongahela, then flowing farther toward the Allegheny and on into the Ohio. And from there perhaps all the way to the Mississippi. And all the while the sunshine warmed her cheeks, and the gentle breeze blew the fear from her bit by bit.

"... and of all the invertebrates, they are the only ones that can distinguish sounds ..."

Gabe talked about insects and bugs and his berm. She was comforted by the sound of his voice.

The morning stretched on into afternoon. Hadley watched a lone water spider struggling against the slow-moving current. She snapped off a long piece of wild grass and guided the spider safely toward some rocks near the bank.

"I'm glad you moved here," said Gabe suddenly.

Hadley looked at him and frowned. She definitely couldn't agree.

"I know this may be really hard for you to believe . . ." Gabe cleared his throat. "But I don't have a whole lot of friends."

Hadley examined Gabe closely—his unkempt hair, his shirt with the stitching on the shoulder coming undone, his filthy fingernails. She knew there weren't many kids who would appreciate his intense interest in dirt and bugs, but once you got past that, Gabe was a pretty nice guy.

"Promise me something?" she said.

"Sure."

"If I did . . . If I was . . . I mean were . . ." Hadley struggled to find the right words. "If I suddenly were to leave without saying goodbye . . . will you promise you'll come looking for me?"

Gabe frowned. "Why? Are you planning on going somewhere?"

"Just promise."

Gabe stared at her for a moment. He opened his mouth as if to say something, and then shut it again. He nodded, and then stood. "I gotta go. Grandma's got a bunch of chores waiting for me."

Having Gabe around made Hadley feel safe. But she didn't know what she could say to make him stay. "I'll help you finish the berm later," she offered.

Gabe grinned. The grass squashed beneath his feet as he turned and strolled back toward the woods. Before he got far, he stopped and looked back. "I almost forgot. Do you still have that eye?"

Hadley flinched. "Yeah. Why?"

"Remember when we were building the berm and your shovel got stuck? Well, I excavated something from the earth—a real archaeological find!"

Hadley was almost afraid to ask. "What was it?"

"An old doll. I think your eye could belong to it. It only has one."

Twenty-nine

I **am sick with worry and fright.** *I do not know what shall become of me. I have pressed my brain all night and all day to figure a way out of my horrific bargain.*

Papa has had his operation and lies in his bed recovering. Doctor Fenton provided him with an adequate dose of ether to dull the pain. Papa is so very brave. He did not cry out once during the procedure. The doctor has instructed Frau Heinzelmann to change Papa's dressing regularly and keep the wound clean. She tosses the old bandages in a waste bin in the kitchen.

I sit at the table clutching the doll Papa made for me what now seems like so long ago. It has been my only comfort since things began to go awry.

"I caught the kobold," I confess to Frau Heinzelmann.

She glances at me and narrows her eyes. I know she does not believe me.

"And how did you accomplish that?" she asks, setting dirty dishes into the washbasin. She has left a paring knife on the table. It sits in front of me, its blade catching the light, gleaming.

"I set a trail of bread crumbs leading from the chimney," I say absentmindedly. I smooth my doll's pretty pink dress. She looks at me with her large glassy eyes.

"And how do you know you caught a kobold, then?" she says, pointing her pudgy finger at me. "The chimney is an unlocked door. A gateway to the unknown. Any number of things may enter through it."

I pause and wonder. Did I in fact catch a kobold? Or is it something much darker?

"You had best be careful," she says. "There are wicked things out there. Things that will not think twice of killing you, tearing out your soul, and keeping it in their pocket like a prize."

My throat goes dry as desert dust. Now more than ever I question all I've done. "B-but... what if I promised this creature something?" I say. "What shall I do then?"

Frau Heinzelmann continues to scour the dishes, pots, and pans while she thinks. "Then," she says finally and resolutely, "like the pretty maiden from Rumpelstiltskin, you must find a way to outsmart it. Trick it, or pay the price."

I think of what the creature has asked of me. I think of

its exact words. *"If you promise to give me something in return..."*

And suddenly, Frau Heinzelmann's words resonate inside me and I have a solution. I know what I must do. I spring to my feet.

"Oh, thank you," I say. "Thank you so very much!"

She smiles at me and shakes her head. And when the woman's back is turned, I snatch up my doll and then tuck something else into the fold of my skirt. I hurry out of the room to summon all my courage and prepare for the dreadful act.

That night I wait for Frau Heinzelmann to leave and for Mama and Papa to sleep. The house moans and groans and I know it is time. I know what must be done, and though it will be so very painful, I must be as brave as Papa, for there is no other way.

I use the knife I pocketed from the kitchen. It takes all my strength and energy to make the extraction, but once I have accomplished the horrid task, I stagger, one step at a time, down the staircase.

I nearly fall twice, but catch myself at the last moment on the railing. My heart thuds in my chest; my insides are like jelly. The blood-soaked bandages are wet against my face and I feel the copper-tasting liquid trickle down my cheek and onto my lips.

I manage to make it to the fireplace, where I drop to the floor, hang my head, and wait. I hold the vile thing in one hand, keeping my fingers clenched tight around it. My stomach churns at the thought.

"Do you have them?" I suddenly hear the creature say. "Do you have the eyes?"

I lift my head, and with my one good eye I see the little girl with the long white hair and black eyes standing before me. She sees my face and snarls. "What's this?"

"I—I promised you something," I choke out. "I did not promise you things. Therefore I only owe you one eye, not two."

I detect a slight quiver in her thin lips as they curl into a malevolent scowl. "Ah, but my meaning was quite clear."

"As were my wishes," I say confidently.

She pauses briefly and then sighs, as though my courage amuses her. "You shall have your way. I shall take the one."

I hold out my hand, my fist clenched tight.

"It is yours," I say firmly, "in fulfillment of my promise. But then we are finished. You must leave this house immediately. For I do not wish to see you—with my one eye—ever again."

Slowly, carefully, I uncurl my fingers. Sitting in the palm of my hand, sparkling in the dying light of the fireplace embers, is an eye. She snatches it up greedily.

"You shall have your final wish!" she says.

As I watch her disappear into the darkness a small smile curls my lips.

Thirty

Her mother's cheerful humming filled the kitchen, but it was no comfort to Hadley. This mother would be as much help as a wax mannequin or a cardboard cutout. Hadley had to get the eye. The eye was the key to all her misery.

It sat on the floor in her bedroom, staring at her. She picked it up carefully and examined it again. The pupil was black and dilated. The blue-gray folds of the iris were quite the opposite of Hadley's deep brown. Did it belong to the old doll in the ravine? Had the old doll belonged to the girl who died?

Hadley looked toward the dollhouse, as though it somehow held the answers to her questions. She swallowed a baseball-sized lump. Her mother's doll sat peacefully in the living room. Granny de Mone lay in the room above the garage. Her father's doll was nowhere to be found. Slowly, she peered around the room, half expecting it to spring out at her from the shadows.

Hadley's fingers tightened around the smooth glass eye before burying it in her pocket. She needed help to sort things out. But who could she turn to? Who was crazy enough to believe her story?

Hadley's spine straightened. "Crazy," she said out loud.

She grabbed a little red purse that hung in her closet and flung the strap over her shoulder. There wasn't much money in it, but it was enough for bus fare to and from the city.

Blood beat hard in her ears as she fled down the steps. She took the last three steps at a jump and landed with a thud in the middle of the hall. The sound echoed through the whole house.

He stood at the far end of the hall. As the shape took form in Hadley's mind, her lips parted and her hand flew to her mouth to stifle the sound.

The figure was twisted and mangled. One arm hung lower than the other. One knee was bent inward and the black suit was tattered and torn. It was like his body had been chewed up and spit out. Like it had been crushed by a garbage truck.

"There you are. I've been looking for you everywhere." He took a jerky step toward her. His jaw swung back and forth, unhinged.

Hadley eyed the door. She turned to make a run for it, but it was as though she was waist-deep in mud. Her feet moved, and everything around her blurred, but the door didn't seem to be getting any closer. Over her shoulder, she could see him limping steadily toward her.

She pressed forward, her muscles on fire, but before she could get halfway to the entrance, a hand grabbed her arm and pulled her back.

"Let go," she growled.

Thrashing and twisting, Hadley managed to break free from his grasp, and though she plunged forward, the front door seemed to move farther away. She lunged for it again, but her foot slipped and she fell flat on the hardwood floor. He snatched her ankle and began dragging her backward a second time.

"Leave me alone!" she screamed, kicking wildly. "Get away!"

His grip tightened.

In the struggle, the eye slipped from her pocket. It rolled out, stopping an arm's length from her face. Without thinking, she scooped it up, words exploding from her lips.

"I wish I'd never met you!"

Hadley's feet kicked and scuffed at the wood floor. She stopped struggling and turned to discover she was alone in the hall.

Blood prickled through the veins in her leg. It was as hollow and numb as her other three limbs. Relieved that she still had control of her body, she scrambled to her feet and bolted through the door.

The sun melted through the trees, sprinkling beads of gold along the street. Hadley raced down the porch steps all the way to the curb. She stared back at the house and suddenly it looked like a giant face—the door was the nose, and the porch an enormous smile of white picket teeth. It grinned at her like it knew something she didn't.

Thirty-one

Hadley **wove briskly** through the side streets until she finally emerged onto Brownsville Road.

The bus stop was crowded. One woman read a magazine. Several others checked their phones. A teenager listened to music with big white headphones. A plane flew low overhead, and in the distance, a siren blared.

In minutes a bus screeched to a halt. A cloud of noxious fumes exploded from the exhaust pipe. Hadley climbed aboard, paid her fare, and slumped into a window seat. The bus lurched forward and the landscape began to slip by. Houses and fields gave way to buildings, shops, and restaurants. It made Hadley feel like she'd been trapped in the old house on Orchard Drive far too long.

In no time, she arrived in the city. She wandered along the familiar streets until she reached her destination. As she stood on the sidewalk staring up at the brown bricks, she heaved a sigh of relief.

The building was a welcoming sight. She stepped through the glass door and into the foyer. She located the name on the index, then pressed the numbers, and a crackly voice burst through the intercom.

"Hello? Who's there? Hello?"

"It's Hadley. I need to see you."

"Hello? I can't hear you. Is someone there?"

"It's me, Hadley," she said, banging her fist on the speaker. The old thing never worked properly. "Can I come up?"

There was a pause and then the buzzer sounded. Hadley snatched the door and headed past the tattered foyer sofa toward the old elevators.

She hit the red up button and the metal doors slid open. Inside the elevator she noticed details she'd overlooked in the past—a crack in the fake wood paneling, an oily black stain on the ceiling, a chip in the plastic third-floor button. The imperfections were strangely comforting.

The hallway was dim, the brown-and-orange carpet worn bare in the center. She almost passed right by Grace's apartment and headed straight into hers—but then she remembered she no longer lived there. The mysterious gnome-and-elevator-hating couple did.

Hadley halted short of Grace's door, keeping well back in

case any invisible gnomes happened to be lounging nearby. Extending her arm as far as she could reach, she knocked gently.

The door flew wildly open. Grace was a blur of color and energy. A crinkly golden skirt flounced beneath a peacock-blue blouse that was just a smidge too tight. Grace's trademark beads swung like pendulums. Today, her Birkenstock sandals were flaming red. As was her hair. Classical music, something vaguely Vivaldi-ish, drifted into the hall.

At first she looked past Hadley, almost through her, as though Hadley were invisible. Then their eyes locked and a large smile seemed to envelop Grace's entire face. She threw her arms around Hadley and squeezed so tight Hadley worried she might crack a rib. Grace released her and stepped back as though to get a more complete look. She peered left and then right, and though there wasn't the least chance of anyone hearing, she leaned forward and whispered, "The gnomes are happy to see you."

Grace took Hadley by the shoulder and yanked her inside. As she stood in the foyer looking on into the living room, it suddenly occurred to Hadley that in all the years she'd lived in the building, she'd never set foot inside Grace's apartment.

The place smelled of gingerbread and old books. Tiny glass bottles that might once have contained perfumes or medicines dangled from the ceiling at various levels, like spiders from spun threads. Some were round, others square, and some even pyramid-shaped. They were as unusual and colorful as the beads around Grace's neck.

Several bottles hung in front of the giant sliding glass door that led out to a balcony, while some were suspended in the archway between the foyer and the living space. Many swayed randomly throughout the apartment, tinkling together softly as though pushed by some mysterious undetectable breeze. Sunlight reflected off and beamed through them, casting a rainbow of colorful spangles on the walls and floor. Most bottles were open, but a few were sealed tight with corks.

"The bottles trick the demons," said Grace, leading Hadley through the space. "Evil spirits are often confused by light and color." She waved her beads and winked knowingly. "They enter the bottles thinking they are entering souls. I cap those quickly, trapping the spirits inside."

Hadley nodded. "Good plan."

With all the recent ripples in Hadley's reality, it was comforting to see Grace hadn't changed. Hadley stepped gingerly through the space, dodging and ducking the bottles—especially the corked ones.

Grace's furniture and knickknacks were a jumble of tastes and styles. An Asian fan hung above a portrait of a young Queen Victoria. Dopey and Grumpy stuffies sat beneath a strangely angled lamp whose base was a replica of the Leaning Tower of Pisa. The coffee table was a giant slab of driftwood with a dainty embroidered chair on one side and a leather one in the shape of a giant baseball mitt on the other. Hadley sank deep into the glove chair, while Grace sat upright on the antique.

"What brings you here?" she said, her eyes bright and bulging behind her large lensless frames. "You look worried. And slightly constipated. I'll get you some prune and acai berry juice."

Before Hadley could stop her, Grace hurried off into the kitchen and returned a few minutes later with a bamboo tray carrying a staggering pile of cucumber and alfalfa sandwiches and a mug brimming with a purplish-brown liquid.

Hadley graciously accepted a sandwich. Together, they crunched loudly on the crusty brown bread and crisp cucumbers. Then Grace handed her a mug. "That's it," she said. "Go on and drink. You'll feel better. And lighter quite soon."

Hadley took a sip. The horridly sour liquid churned in her stomach. She made a face and put down the mug, gathering her thoughts.

"Now, tell me," said Grace. "What's troubling you?"

Hadley took a deep breath, and then, like a great dam had burst inside her, her story gushed forth in a giant frothy wave of words. There was no particular order to the events. She mentioned her real father, Ed's disappearance, Isaac's torn ligaments, her mother's strange behavior, and the dollhouse she could not get rid of. She ended her incoherent rant by taking out the glass eye and holding it up to the light.

"I found this. It's magic. I think it grants wishes."

Grace leaned far back in her chair, placing as much distance as possible between herself and the eye, as though it were some kind of ancient evil. For the first time Hadley could remember, Grace frowned.

"I warned you," she said quietly. "Wishes come with a cost."

Her words stirred inside Hadley. "I know that now. But I didn't know I was doing it at first. It all just seemed to slip so easily out of me and then, it, well, sort of spiraled out of control."

Grace's eyes crinkled with a hint of resigned sadness. "Yes. Wishes have a way of doing that."

"So, you believe me, then?"

Grace looked Hadley firmly in the eye. "Of course. I believe you believe."

Hadley deflated slightly. "That's not the same thing."

"Ah," said Grace. "But it is. You see, there is no one giant hard-and-fast reality. Life is billions of minute and fluid realities bumping into each other and connecting for brief moments in time. Your reality is not mine. But then, mine is not yours. So yes—yes, I believe you because you believe you."

It wasn't the same thing, but Hadley decided it was the best she would get.

"Well then, do you think I can undo what I've done? Do you think there's a way to get back what I've lost?"

The woman placed one foot across her knee, folded her arms and raised her chin. She looked like she was posing for a statue. She seemed to think for a very long time and then she said, "I'm not sure. Some things, I'm afraid, can never be undone."

Hadley sank lower into the squishy leather glove as though the weight of the world were pressing her down.

Then Grace held up an aha index finger. "Though, perhaps," she said, with a sudden cheerfulness that startled Hadley, "perhaps if you give something back. Perhaps if you *give* rather than *take*. That might be the answer. Do you know where the eye belongs? Could you return it to its owner?"

Hadley sat up straight. Her eyes grew saucer-wide. The old doll—the one Gabe had found. It was missing an eye. That's where the eye belonged. Maybe if she returned the eye to the doll, she'd get back everything she'd lost. She nodded fiercely. "I think I might. If I return the eye, things might go back to the way they were. Back to normal."

Grace stood. She placed a gentle hand on Hadley's shoulder. "I dislike that word."

"What word?"

"Normal." Grace made a face as though she'd tasted something bitter. "What is *normal* depends on how you look at things. Like beauty, and love, and happiness—it's all about perspective."

"Huh?" said Hadley.

"Well," said Grace thoughtfully. "If you believe someone is beautiful, then who is to tell you they are not? And if you believe you are happy, then aren't you?"

Hadley thought about this for a second. Some people were perpetually miserable. Others always happy. It didn't matter what was happening in their lives—some people just chose to be happy.

"So, if I believe I'm happy, I will be?" said Hadley.

"Exactly."

Hadley stood. The Vivaldi music had ended. It was time to go.

"The gnomes—they like you," said Grace. "They told me to tell you." She took off her glasses. Her eyes seemed much smaller without the frames. Less bright. "They say you can stay here if you like. But if you choose to go back you must be careful. There are things out there. Terrible things. Things that will steal your soul and hold on to it forever."

The warning sent tremors quaking up Hadley's spine. Grace's apartment was warm. It was kooky, but comfortable. Part of Hadley wanted to stay there and never return to the old house. But how could she leave her mother? She couldn't abandon her and Ed and Isaac. She had to at least try to set things right.

Before she left the comfort of the gingerbread scent and the tiny tinkling of the glass bottles, she paused in the doorway. "If I should somehow, well . . . *disappear* . . . will you remember me? Will you come look for me?"

Grace reached for Hadley and gave her a tight squeeze. "I'll send the gnomes."

Thirty-two

Yellow clouds clotted the sky above, not so much gathering as growing and thickening in every direction. They blotted out the setting sun and seemed to be descending, closing in around the neighborhood.

Hadley stared at the house from the curb. She looked at it as if for the very first time. It was tall and majestic, yet whitewashed in a lazy sort of indifference that came with age. She had never noticed just how beautiful it really was. Elegant and lofty—the sort of house anyone would love to call home. Anyone who didn't know its secret.

But Hadley did know. She knew there was more than wood and brick and mortar holding it together. There was something else—and it was evil.

Hadley clenched her fists and moved steadily toward the front door. A strange sense of peace welled within her—the kind of peace that came with purpose, with the simple knowledge of what must be done.

The foyer was dark. And cold. And the silence that greeted her was so thick and complete it was as though she'd entered a tomb.

"Mom?" she called. Her voice quivered slightly as it rippled through the stillness. "Are you there?"

The kitchen was empty. Not only was there no sign of her mother, the jars that usually lined the countertop were missing, as was the dish towel that had hung from the stove handle. Hadley opened the cupboards one by one and then the drawers—even the fridge. All were bare.

She searched the dining room next, and then the living room. All the while she called out, "Mom? Where are you?" Each room seemed emptier than the previous, the stillness spreading like black mold.

Where was her mother? Had she gone looking for Hadley? Where was all the food? All their household things?

A warning thudded in Hadley's chest. She did her best to ignore it and pressed on. She needed to find her mother. She needed to tell her the whole story. Together they'd replace the eye. They'd get Ed and Isaac back. And then maybe, just maybe, they could all leave the house forever.

Hadley climbed the steps. The door to her bedroom was ajar. Hadley could see the pink organza dress from the hallway. It lay across her bed as though it had been placed there for her to wear once again.

Anger churned inside her. That dress—that hideous dress. She burst into her room, snatched up the frilly pink fabric, and threw open her closet. The dress slipped from her fingers and fluttered to the floor. Her clothes were gone. They had disappeared along with everything else. The old furniture was intact, the furniture that had never quite belonged to her, but all her things, her unpacked boxes of junk, were missing. Even the dollhouse was gone.

"The dollhouse." She gulped. She needed to find it.

Her heart beat wildly in her throat as she raced down the hallway and up the narrow steps leading to the attic. The old clutter lay under thick dust and yellowing sheets as though it had never been disturbed. Hadley flung one of the sheets aside and located the dollhouse. It was in the exact spot she'd first found it.

Her eyes flitted from room to room, searching each space. Nothing was unusual. Nothing had changed. Everything was in its place. And then it hit her. It wasn't what was in the dollhouse but what wasn't that sent an electric shock pulsing through her veins, zipping toward her heart.

She reached into her pocket and pulled out the eye. Gabe. She had to find him, and quickly. She had to get the old one-eyed doll from him. She had to return the missing eye to it before it was too late.

Hadley's arms and legs felt stranger than ever as she left the house and ran into the yard.

The yellowish mist had descended on the house and was growing thicker by the minute. It seemed to press down on her, making it harder and harder to breathe. Hadley couldn't see beyond the property's edge. It was as if the street, the trees, the other houses lay somewhere beyond the fog, just out of reach.

She stood at the edge of the ravine, fanning the air side to side. Each time she managed to move a bit of fog it was closed back in like curtains flopping back into place. "Gabe!" she cried. "Are you there? Gabe!" A river of relief washed over her when she heard his voice.

"Hadley? Is that you? Where are you?"

"I'm here, Gabe! I need your help!"

"Just a sec," he said. "I'm coming."

"Do you have the doll?" she yelled. "Tell me you still have it!"

"It's at home," he said. "Why?"

Gabe's voice drew nearer. He must have been only a few feet away. Hadley swatted again at the yellow fog, but it was no use. It was like trying to part water.

"Don't come any closer," she yelled. "I need you to get the doll. Get it now and bring it here. We need to put back the eye!"

"What? Why?"

"Just do it," she said. "And hurry. Before it's too late."

Hadley could hear Gabe drop his shovel. She felt he was so close, if she could just reach through, she could touch him.

"Is everything okay?" He sounded worried.

"No—it's not! Please, Gabe. Hurry!"

"Okay," he said. "Wait right there. I'll be right back. Don't go anywhere!"

Seconds passed like hours. The fog was so thick and so tight it was growing harder to breathe. Hadley swallowed great gulps, but her lungs began to ache under the strain.

Then the door to the apartment above the garage swung open. Althea de Mone waved at Hadley. "I'm so glad I found you!" she said. "I've been looking all over! You must come inside."

Hadley searched frantically for Gabe, trying once again to see beyond the fog, certain he would arrive any moment. "Not now, Granny. I'm busy."

"But it's finally ready," she said cheerfully. "Don't you want to see it?"

Hadley turned to face the old woman.

Althea de Mone stood at the top of the metal stairs. She held something in her hands. "Your gift, dear," she said. "I think you'll like it." And then she disappeared inside.

Thirty-three

Hadley paced steadily toward the garage. She grasped the metal railing, and as she climbed the steps she found herself thinking of an old poem she'd once read, the one that began: *Will you walk into my parlour? said the Spider to the Fly . . .*

The door was wide open. Granny sat on the floral sofa, a cup of steaming tea halfway to her lips. Her dark glasses obscured her eyes, but something told Hadley the old woman was looking right at her.

As Hadley stepped inside, a thin grin snaked across Granny's lips. She took a sip of tea and then gently lowered the cup, placing it on its saucer.

"Come in, dear," she said quietly. She patted the empty space on the sofa beside her. Facedown in her lap was a doll.

"I can't stay," said Hadley, shifting nervously, checking through the open door for Gabe. "I've got something really important I need to do."

"But you have something important to do right here," she said. "Come sit with me. I have something to tell you. There's more to that old story. Do you want to hear?"

"I can't, Granny, I—" she tried to explain. The eye bulged in her pocket; her hand flew to it instinctively. She should go back outside. Gabe would be there by now—with the doll.

"He's not coming," Granny said quietly.

"Who?" asked Hadley, still searching through the open door.

"Why, that friend of yours—Gabe—isn't that who you're looking for?"

Hadley took a tentative step toward the sofa. "But how ..."

"Have some tea," said Granny, pouring a cup.

Hadley shook her head slowly. Something had changed. The tea no longer smelled fresh and soothing. It smelled musky and earthy like boiled dirt.

Hadley stared at the doll in Granny's lap. It wore a pink frilly dress identical to the one she'd been forced to wear. Identical to the one the first doll had worn.

"That girl," said Granny, "the one who died all those

years ago. She was such a charming little thing—and feisty, just like you. But so unhappy. So terribly unhappy. How she'd longed to have both her parents by her side. How she'd longed to return to her old home. How she'd wished for a friend . . ."

"I'm sorry, Granny. I really don't have time for this right now," said Hadley. "I've got to go . . ."

"She fell down the stairs one night, poor dear. They buried her at the back of the yard—to keep her near the house."

Granny's words reached Hadley's ears in good time, but they seemed to take a lot longer to sink into her brain. The girl fell down the stairs. The scream. The girl's scream. The one she'd heard in the house the day Isaac hurt his ankle . . .

"Of course, the yard was much larger in those days," she went on. "With all the erosion of soil it's dropped off now. The grave has slid right down into the ravine."

Gabe was right. The soil was eroding. And the doll they found—had it been buried along with the girl? Was there a grave somewhere down there? A box of bones long decomposed? Did all those flesh flies still think there was a body somewhere to feast on? Was that why they hung around? Or were there more bodies? Fresh bodies, bodies of missing families . . .

Hadley gulped.

"Her name was Althea," said the old woman. "Did I mention that?"

"B-but," Hadley stammered, somehow unable to connect the words with their meaning, "isn't that *your* name?"

Light from the open door cast a shadow on the heavy dark drapes behind the old woman. The proportions of her body were wrong—the head too large and angular and the body too thin. It looked like some kind of—

Before the word had fully formed in her mind, Hadley saw Granny's name as if it were written in the air above her. Althea S. de Mone . . .

Althea's demon.

Hadley drew in her breath as the door slammed shut behind her. She spun around and tugged at it, but it was sealed tight.

"Such a sweet little girl," continued the old woman. "And clever, too."

Hadley stared into the dark glasses. Grace's words echoed in her mind. *Perhaps if you give rather than take . . .*

She was suddenly certain that what lay behind the dark glasses was a great gaping hole in place of an eye. That was where the glass eye belonged. Hadley had to replace it—to break the spell.

In a burst of energy, she lunged for the sofa, and before

the old woman could react, Hadley had snatched the frames and yanked them from her face.

Althea de Mone did not move a muscle. She simply sat staring calmly at Hadley. Her two eyes were enormous, completely black and unblinking. Like an insect.

Hadley shrank back. The glasses clanged to the ground. The woman's lips curled into a crooked smile. Hadley hadn't noticed before how sharp her tiny white teeth appeared.

"She tricked me, you know," said the old woman matter-of-factly. "I gave her all she'd asked for—even her final wish, to never see me again—and how did she repay me? With treachery. She was to give me one small thing in return—one of her precious little eyes. But when the time came, I received a glass imitation."

Hadley's hand flew to her pocket once again. The eye was still there. "Wh-who are you? What are you really?"

"What does it matter?" she said. "'A rose is a rose . . .'"

Hadley needed to get out of the apartment. She needed to find Gabe. She needed to get her hands on the one-eyed doll.

"How Althea loved her dollhouse. And her dolls. That's what gave me the idea. To make the dolls."

Thunk.

Hadley had heard that sound before. She searched the apartment, her eyes settling on the old trunk in the far corner.

The woman stood and walked calmly toward it. Holding the new doll in one hand, she lifted the lid.

Hadley's heart nearly stopped as her world narrowed to a fine point.

In the trunk lay row upon row of wooden dolls—dolls of all shapes and sizes—male and female, old and young. They had large, vacant eyes.

Hadley's insides turned to stone. Lying there, as if in a tomb, was the first family of dolls—the one with the little girl   the family from the newspaper, the one that had gone missing from the house. Beside them was Hadley's father, a creepy smile still fixed to his lips. And then she saw them—Ed, Isaac . . . and her mother.

"Lovely," Granny said, "don't you think?"

Seeing Ed, Isaac, and her mother lying there sparked courage in Hadley. She raised herself taller and squared her shoulders. She met the demon's black eyes with a fierce scowl. "I want them back," she said coldly.

"Ah, but you gave them to me," she said, chuckling. "Don't you recall?"

Hadley fished through her memory. What did the old woman mean? Then suddenly she recalled her wish. Up in the attic. *I wish my family were like these dolls.*

Hadley closed her eyes. She had said that. She had wished it. But she hadn't meant it. Not that way. Without thinking, she pulled out the glass eye.

"That's it," said the old woman. "You have one wish left. Go on. Make it a good one."

The words flew out of Hadley's mouth before she could stop them. "I want my family back."

As the final word left her lips, the old woman's grin grew frighteningly wide. Hadley could feel the blood crackling to a halt inside her chest. The eye slipped from her hand and rolled across the floor. The numbness was traveling from Hadley's heart toward her head. Once it reached her brain she would not be able to control her body.

If you get something, you must give something in return...

The old woman stooped to retrieve the eye. She held it up to the dark bulb that was her own. "Ah, the falseness of it all. The constant reminder of the treachery I suffered. I vowed never to be fooled again. Never to rely on promises. Now I take what I'm owed. Limb by precious limb..."

She extended the doll she had been holding and Hadley got a clear view of the wooden face with large, pleading eyes. It looked exactly like Hadley.

Hadley backed away. She turned and staggered toward the window. She had to get out of the apartment before it was too late. The window was her only hope. If she could smash it, she could escape. It wasn't too high up. She could jump out the window and get away. She grabbed the dark drapes and yanked. The curtains ripped off their rod and dropped to the ground.

A giant metal rim with spokes filled the space outside the window. Behind the huge wheel was a rocking chair the size of a mountain.

Thirty-four

The August humidity had eased. Summer was fading fast and autumn lay just around the corner. The downward arc of the calendar had begun.

In Hays Woods the canopy was changing from deep green to crimson and gold. Flies still buzzed about during the day, but they retreated when night came—and it came earlier these days. The woods were quieter now as well— the birds had begun to fly south. The snakes and rodents had disappeared into their nests.

Hadley lay on her bed, staring at the ceiling. The pink organza dress no longer itched. It fit perfectly. It was as though by wearing it, she had finally become the person she was meant to be.

Ed and Mom sat facing each other in the family room. They were smiling. They were happy again at last. Isaac was at the kitchen table in front of a bowl heaped with Flaxy O's.

Hadley's final wish had come true after all. They were all together again. The perfect family. In the perfect house. How could she ever have wanted anything else?

Outside, the sky was a pale, lackluster yellow—the color of an old sheet gathering dust. And somewhere, in the vast space beyond, was Gabe.

Had he come to rescue her with the one-eyed doll after all? Had he wondered where she'd gone? Was he worried about her now? If only she had waited a minute longer. If only...

Hadley imagined Gabe in Hays Woods, looking through his binoculars, searching for bugs, or lingering snakes and birds. She hoped he had finished building the retaining wall. She hoped he would build the berm that would redirect the water flow. If not, the house would eventually drop off into the ravine like he'd said.

Maybe Gabe would remember her—remember what to do with the one-eyed doll. Maybe he'd come looking for her. Maybe he'd bring the doll, return the eye, and break the spell. She could no longer go to Gabe, but there was nothing stopping Gabe from coming to her. If he remembered.

Hadley wished Gabe was with her now. She wished very hard, only she had nothing left to pay with, so there were no more wishes to be had. Grace had warned her. Hadley hadn't listened.

Of course Grace might remember as well. She might come by the house looking for her, too. She could bring her carpetbag purse filled with her special tools—the feather duster and alluvial mud. Perhaps she could capture the old demon in one of her colorful glass bottles and cork it tight. She might even send the invisible gnomes. Perhaps invisible gnomes could fight demons. After all, they'd liked her. Grace had said so.

As Hadley lay still and calm, she was reminded of something else Grace had told her. *If you believe you are happy, then aren't you?* Hadley had her family back. They were all together now. Forever. And though not in the way she'd hoped, she decided it was okay. She was happy.

Suddenly, a shadow crept over her. The yellow sheet flew away and the dollhouse exploded with bright light. Fingers tightened around Hadley's body as she was lifted gently into the air. Large eyes stared at her in surprise and wonder.

Then a low rumble echoed across the floor. It was the eye. The girl picked it up and held it beside Hadley's head.

Hadley tried desperately to move her mouth—to warn the girl—but her tongue was like stone. Her body was its own prison.

Inside her head, words danced themselves into a feverish

frenzy. They screamed this way and that, trying desperately to find a way out. They bounced off the walls of her mind, echoing on and on, until they disappeared.

I'm not a doll.
I'm not a doll.
I'm not a doll . . .

ACKNOWLEDGMENTS

When I was in the seventh grade, the local high school, Wexford Collegiate, put on a performance of *The Monkey's Paw* and invited surrounding elementary schools to attend. I would like to thank my teachers for taking our class to see the play. I would also like to thank author W. W. Jacobs for never showing me what stood behind that door. The gentle *knock, knock, knock* has echoed in my mind all these years.

I completed the first draft of this manuscript several years ago, and it's not without the help and support of many wonderful people that it shifted and morphed and changed until it found its true shape.

A heartfelt thank-you to my first-draft readers—Valerie Sherrard, Martha Martin, Deborah Kerbel, Kathy Temean, and Jaime Cohen. Thank you to Alison Weiss, whose feedback led to valuable changes. Thank you to Caroline Carlson for helping me navigate the Pittsburgh area, and to Darlene Beck Jacobson for lending me her historical fiction eyes.

Thank you to the Ontario Arts Council for your generous support of this work via the Writers' Reserve Program.

Thank you to the very talented Nicoletta Ceccoli for the delightfully creepy cover and illustrations.

To my three wonderful children and to my amazing husband, Michael Cohen—your love and support mean the world to me. Always.

To my superhero agent, John M. Cusick—I'm so very lucky that something about this story snagged your attention all those years ago, and that you stuck with it and me on our long journey to this great place.

And last, but most important on this list, the biggest thank-you goes to the amazing team at Roaring Brook Press—to Anne Diebel for her wonderful design, to Karla Reganold and her copyediting team, who made sure all my "eyes" are dotted, and especially to my brilliant editor, Emily Feinberg, whose keen eyes, patience, and absolute dedication have made this book the very best it can be.

Check out other spooky books
by
MARINA COHEN

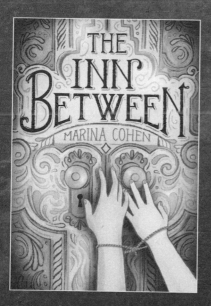